LOVE BEFORE
&
AFTER CORONA

Mukulika Basu

BlueRose ONE.com
Stories Matter
NewDelhi • London

BLUEROSE PUBLISHERS
India | U.K.

BlueRose ONE

For permissions requests or inquiries regarding this publication, please contact:

BLUEROSE PUBLISHERS
www.BlueRoseONE.com
info@bluerosepublishers.com
+91 8882 898 898
+4407342408967

ISBN: 978-93-7542-140-5

Cover Design: Mukulika Basu
Typesetting: Manisha Rawat

First Edition: February 2026

Dedication

To my mother Malavika Basu Das and
father Asim Kumar Basu

Acknowledgement

I love to dream. I love to think. I love to write. I feel my writing is mirror of my mind. Many thoughts came in my mind and sometimes imaginations were mixed with those thoughts. My writing was started from that time. I try to send social messages through my writing. I love to make friendship with people. So I thought to share my writing with others. Thanks to God for giving me this life and blessing me always. Thanks to my mother and father for their love, blessings, teachings, support and encouragement. Thanks to my all relatives, friends, neighbours and well-wishers. Thanks to entire team of BlueRose Publishers for giving me this opportunity to publish this book. Thanks to all persons who are related with this book and last but not least thanks to all my readers in advance. This book is for 'You.'

About The Author

Dr. Mukulika Basu is a friendly and fun-loving person. She is from Kolkata and is a Graduate in English. She is fond of writing since childhood. Her writings have been published in several newspapers and magazines. She wrote three books before. Love Before & After Corona is her third novel and fifth book. Her first book came out in 2012 at the Kolkata Book Fair. Her second book came out in 2017 and her third book came out in 2018 and her fourth book came out in 2025. Writings about her were published in papers and magazines. She got 'Best Writer' award. Writing is her passion. She loves painting and enjoys chess and badminton. Trying her hand at various culinary challenges is also something she is really fond of. She works in occult field also. Her friends say she is genius, she has a good heart just like the open sky and that she is different. She loves to spend time with her family and friends.

Contents

1

∞

Manjulika entered into her bedroom. She closed the door, took out packet of 'Freedom Friendly' sanitary napkin. It was her second day of period and she had only one sanitary napkin. She kept the packet inside wardrobe and changed dress and found Kajal was calling her, Manjulika received the call, 'Hello!'

'Hello, what are you doing?'

Manjulika took a pause and said, 'I just returned from shop. Went to buy a talcum powder.' Manjulika's friend Kajal was she-male, a person of third-gender, had not any experience about period so Manjulika had not discussed any matter related to period with her.

'Oh which brand?'

'Romantic.' Manjulika said and sat on bed.

'Oho Romantic? Thinking about whom? Gautam?'

'Don't take his name. He is just disgusting.' Manjulika said with little angry expression. Gautam was Manjulika's office collogue who had proposed Manjulika before two months and Manjulika had rejected him very politely but he was continuing disturbing her. Kajal said, 'Really he is not doing good. Still does he disturb you?'

'Don't ask. Even today he messaged me in morning.'

'What message?'

'Good morning. How are you? For two days I can't see you. I miss a you lot.' Manjulika said again, 'Last weekend also he messaged me.'

'Oh, very romantic but he should not disturb you when you don't like him.'

'I wanted to keep friendship but after this kind behavior I don't want to keep that also.'

'Leave it.'

'Sure and to buy romantic powder I don't have to be in love with someone. I am in love with the concept of love and till now and I am in love with myself. I am narcissist.'

'I know those things very well. I was just kidding. I know you bought romantic powder because you are very romantic.'

'Exactly.'

'Anyway don't forget your friend, being romantic. I have called to make a plan for doing our home-party one day. For a long time, we have not done.'

'Yes why not? Really have not met for a long time.'

'Okay let's take Sobha on conference call. Wait I am calling her.'

'Okay.'

After some time Manjulika heard Sobha's voice, 'Hello!' Then she heard Kajal's voice, 'Hello Sobha it is conference call. Manjulika is also on line.'

'Hello Sobha.' Manjulika said.

'Hello Manjulika.'

'Kajal is telling let's meet one day.' Manjulika said.

'Yes let's do our home party. I was also thinking for some days for a long-time we have not done home-party.' Sobha replied.

'Yes I was telling the same to Kajal.' Manjulika replied.

'Okay next Sunday?' Kajal asked.

'Yes why not?' Sobha replied.

They three continued talking for almost thirty minutes more and finally stopped when Manjulika realized ten minutes were left for her regular lunch time and she did not take bath till that time. After cutting the call Manjulika took bath and went to do lunch. Manjulika found her mother Rita and elder sister Madhulika were sitting in dining-place. Manjulika went near dining-table and sat on a chair and said, 'Oh Didi finally after a long time we three are doing lunch together.' Rita smiled and left for kitchen.

'Yes today I have a leave. I really needed it for a long time.'

Manjulika smiled.

'I should not be happy but I am feeling happy that I am getting a leave for my colleague's death.' Madhulika said.

'You are happy for getting leave not for colleague's death. Don't feel guilty.'

'Right.'

'Busy and stressful life is making us selfish.'

'Right.'

Rita came from kitchen.

Maid of Manjulika's home Mithu served rice. Madhulika asked, 'What is made today, Maa? Last Friday we decided Chicken Tikka Butter Masala.'

'Yes Mithu has made.' Rita replied.

'Have you kept some tikka or all have used in gravy?' Manjulika asked looking at Mithu.

'No no I have kept.' Mithu replied and started to serve vegetable items of raw Papaya on Rita's plate and as tried to serve on

Manjulika's plate she said, 'No Mashi don't give me vegetables today. Today chicken is made, give me that and chicken tikka only. You know very well I don't eat anything else than chicken when chicken is made.'

'It's a very bad habit Manju.' Rita said.

'Oh common Maa. Sunday means fun-day. No vegetables today.' Manjulika said as Mithu gave some vegetables on Madhulika's plate.

'I think we should make a rule. As no non-veg on Saturday just like that no veg on Sunday.' Manjulika said.

'Very funny. I also had this kind of habit in teenage. Now it is totally changed. You also should change now.' Madhulika said.

'I can't change at least this habit for Sunday and I regular take fruits, and enough water.' Manjulika said.

'You can't change any habit. That is the truth, like using mobile a lot, waking up late and eating lot of junk-foods.' Rita said. Mithu gave chicken tikka and chicken tikka butter masala to everyone. Manjulika put one piece of chicken tikka in mouth and said, 'Oh nice. Mashi you really have leant to make tikka properly in two attempts.'

Mithu smiled.

'Really tikka tastes really good.' Madhulika said.

'Actually the same taste can't come from OTG or microwave which comes from gas-tandoor.' Manjulika said.

'Really.' Madhulika said again, 'Remember last year's bar-b-que party. Almost same taste like bar-b-que has come.'

'Right.' Manjulika replied and suddenly looked at her mother and said, 'Maa where is Baba?'

'He has eaten earlier. He has meeting in club for next function at 4pm. He wanted to take rest.' Rita said.

'Oh yes function time has come. When is function?' Madhulika asked.

'I also don't know properly. Your Baba was telling two-three months later. He was asking Madhulika you would sing or not.'

'Let's see. I have big problem for leave. For a long time, I don't even practice. Manju will you recite your poetry this year also?' Madhulika said.

'Yes planning. Let's see.' Manjulika replied.

'Have you written anything new? Because all day you are busy with mobile when you stay at home.' Rita said.

'Oh Maa these days I don't spend that much time with mobile.' Manjulika replied.

'Yes always you say that. What have you written in these days?' Rita asked.

'Maa poetry can be written only when it comes in mind, okay.'

'If you are always busy with mobile and never thinks emotionally or never try to write poetry then poetry will not come in your mind automatically.' Rita said.

'Maa poetry comes spontaneously.' Manjulika said.

'To let it come you have to make your mind free.' Rita said.

'Maa come on stop this. Let's enjoy today's lunch.' Manjulika said.

'You always ask me to stop.' Rita said and continued eating.

'Anyway let's make a plan for small trip. I really want to relax for some days. I can manage in next of next weekend.' Madhulika said.

'Really it's needed.' Manjulika said.

'You know Manju when I was discussing about going for tour with Dr. Shefali, and our neighbor Rina Kakima visited our hospital today, she heard that.' Madhulika said.

'Oh no that back-biting Rina Kakima? Why?' Manjulika asked.

'You don't know? She regularly visits these days. She has some problems now in her neck.' Madhulika replied.

'Oh doing that much back-biting she has gotten this problem.' Manjulika said and giggled.

Madhulika smiled. Manjulika asked, 'Anyway what did she say?'

'She asked for how many days you are going for tour?' Madhulika said.

'Then?'

'I said may be for six-seven days, not planned yet.'

'She said oh six-seven days, long time.'

Manjulika giggled. 'Don't laugh. I was feeling an urge to hit her.' Madhulika said. Manjulika giggled more. Madhulika said, 'Then she said, you are in our neighbourhood so we feel relaxed, at least one Dr. is in our neighbourhood, whenever we need we can call you.'

'Oh.' Manjulika replied.

'As if there is no other Dr. in local area and I don't need to be relaxed. How do I treat patients properly if I don't be relaxed? And even I don't have to think there is any other Dr. or not in local area.'

'What did you tell her?' Manjulika asked.

'I said I also need to be relaxed. She gave an idiotic smile. I don't think she understood what I had said.'

'Of-course not. Those kinds of people never understand. Those people who have some depth in mind only they can understand this.' Manjulika said and put one piece of chicken tikka in mouth.

They three continued talking and finished eating. Manjulika went to bedroom and lied and opened Facebook. Manjulika found three friend requests, five messages, forty-five notifications were there.

Manjulika opened notification list, saw once and opened message box. First message was from her one good friend Sunil Kumar from Delhi, which had come at 9.00 a.m. of morning, 'Good morning!'

Manjulika replied, 'Good afternoon!'

Next message, 'Hi dear how r u' was from Arun Kumar, one friend from Manjulika's friend-list. Though Manjulika never considered him as friend. After three days' chatting he had proposed Manjulika, Manjulika had said she treats him like friend, but he had continued forcing her and Manjulika had stopped replying after some days. Manjulika ignored his message and checked next message. It was from her Romanian friend, Daniel Marius, 'Hello niece, how are you? Have a blessed Sunday.'

'I am fine Uncle and you? Have a blessed Sunday.'

Next message was from her friend Laali from Uganda, 'Hi dear how are you doing?' Manjulika replied, 'Fine and how are you? Where are you now? Are you in Uganda or have left for job to other country?'

Laali's reply came, 'No still at my home. Will go soon.'

'How are your two sons and one daughter?'

'They are fine. How is everyone at your home?'

'Fine.'

'How is going your job?'

'Going okay. You know last week I tried Peanut Butter Chicken according to recipe.'

'Oh how was it?'

'I think taste was okay but authentic taste came or not I don't know.'

'Understand.'

Manjulika sent a smiley.

'You know I also tried one Indian item.' Message came from Laali.

'What?'

'Indian Dum Aloo.'

'Oh really?'

'Yes.'

'Do you like it?'

'Very much.'

'I also like but I don't like veg items too much.'

'I also don't like few veg items too much but I liked that.'

'Okay.'

'Oh I heard people of your country like veg items a lot. Even some like veg more than non-veg.'

'Yes.'

'And some even don't eat veg at all for belief?'

'Yes some don't eat for belief.'

'Can you tell me what kind of reason is it?'

'Hard to make you understand. Actually some people think it is not right to kill animals for eating. Some even think it is a sin.'

'What sin? Don't we kill mosquitoes or cockroach?'

'It is their personal belief and some don't kill insects also I think.'

'Really surprising.'

Manjulika smiled and wrote, 'But some say insects disturb us so we kill.'

'But will they kill human if any human being will disturb them? If there will be no chance of arrest, then even will they kill just being disturbed? That means they also make difference?'

Manjulika smiled and wrote, 'Nice logic and some of them actually just can't think to eat non-veg. Non-veg is not in food-habit.'

'You are not belonging from different belief?'

'No many people from our belief think like this. But many people eat non-veg, and some of them eat veg only in religious days. Here are other beliefs too which are from our country and many of them don't eat non-veg from those beliefs too.'

'Do you eat non-veg regularly?'

'Sure but in some religious days I eat veg. I did not have this habit before, only my mother followed but in some religious days me and my Didi are also following now.'

'Your elder sister?'

'Yes.'

'Okay dear I have to go to market. Will chat later. Bye.'

'Okay bye.' Manjulika replied and started to check friend requests, opened the first profile and found it was locked. She had never accepted any friend request from any locked profile. She did not respond and saw next profile and found one sketch of almost naked boy and girl in profile picture. Manjulika did not respond and checked third profile and found one boy named Alberto Magnani from Italy. Manjulika always had very big interest to make friendship with people of other countries and beliefs. Manjulika watched the profile properly and accepted the friend request and opened you tube and watched two videos of her most favourite reality show Super Boss where getting a chance was one dream of Manjulika's life. Then she opened one other video and started to watch. The video was a program of a religious scholar. He was doing a stage program and one boy was asking him a question, 'Hi sir, I am Manoj Sharma from Patna. I have a question.'

'Yes brother.'

'Sir you say idol worshipping is wrong and making anyone or anything partner of God is wrong.'

The religious speaker nodded. The boy continued, 'Then keeping any object related to religion is equally wrong, right? If any person is keeping any wooden piece where hundred names of God of your religion are written or any photo where some lines of your religious book is written or any photo of any statue which is related to your belief and the person is thinking his home can be more protected from danger for keeping these kinds of photos, is it not wrong?'

The religious speaker stood up and went near the mike. He started to speak, 'The brother has asked a very good question. If idol worshipping is wrong, then keeping any religious object is wrong or not?'

The boy named Manoj nodded. The religious speaker started to tell again, 'Listen brother the main fact is God is one and you have to believe in God only. We don't worship those things as God. Keeping those things at home are not compulsory also. We believe in one God only. Clear brother?'

'Not at all sir. I think keeping anything at home is not compulsory in our belief also. Even idol worshipping is also not compulsory at all in our belief also. Our belief says there is no particular way of worshipping. In our religious book it is written that how you want you can call God. If you have true believe in God, in which way you call God, God will accept your prayer.'

'Listen brother God has made a particular rule for it. Everyone has to call him in which way he wants. God has chosen only one belief which has to be followed.'

'Sir my point is if making any person or anything partner of God is wrong then any belief should not have any religious things other than religious book. If any person is keeping any particular religious statue or photo at home or in car and knowingly or unknowingly the person is thinking the statue or photo can favour him that is wrong. Right? And if keeping those things are right then what is wrong if people of any belief worship God in shape of human and that is also not compulsory. At least people of our belief don't cheat themselves. What they do they do it consciously. Sometimes physical representation is needed for mental satisfaction for some people. Every way is not suitable for everyone.'

'Listen brother for mental satisfaction physical representation is not needed. Your faith in God is needed. It is written in book of your belief also that God has no image, no photo, no statue.'

'You said half truth and try to convert people of our belief. It is written in our belief that God has no photo, no image, no statue but is it not written making any photo, image or statue of God and worshipping God through that is wrong. I read it is also written in an explanation that worshipping God without idol is better but worshipping God with idols is not totally worthless. Physical representation or idol worshipping is not compulsory in our belief also. Our belief has every way. If you want to worship God with idol you can do it or if you want to worship God without idol you can do that also just praying to God without idol. There is another way. To worship God without idol no one has to go in other belief. Some people don't know the proper truth and you convert them into your belief using your clever tactics. And why are you taking help of our book to convert people of other belief?'

'Listen brother you have asked me a question and I have given you answer. You are satisfied or not with this answer that is up to you. It is not a place for debt. If you want that we can arrange that later.'

The anchor of that show, 'Okay I think this conversation is done. We should call next person.'

The boy smiled tauntingly and said, 'Okay thank you.' and left.

Manjulika smiled and read one comment, 'Smart boy nailed the joker.' and saw one message came from Alberto Magnani, 'Hi!'

Manjulika replied, 'Hi!'

'Thanks a lot for accepting my friend request beautiful.'

'Welcome and thanks'

'Are you from India?'

'Yes and you?'

'Italy.'

'From which place?' Though Manjulika already had seen those information in Alberto's profile but asked to continue chatting. Alberto replied, 'I am from Rome.'

'I heard nice place. One of my friend visited last year.'

'Thanks dear.'

'What do you do?'

'I have business of leather.'

'Leather business? Italian leather is famous.'

'Yes sure.'

'My friend gifted me a key-ring with Italian leather when she visited Italy.'

'Oh we also sale key-ring and belt but mainly bags and wallets and purses.'

'Nice.'

'So what do you do dear?'

'I am journalist. I work as journalist in T.V. channel of Kolkata.'

'Wow nice profession and Kolkata? Nice city. Once it was capital of India right?'

'You know that also?'

'Actually I have one Bengali friend here. He is my neighbor and does job here. He told many things about Kolkata.'

'Nice.'

'He is doing job here for five years and now he is planning to settle here because he is in love with one female neighbor.'

'Nice.'

'Really I also found very interesting.'

'What is name of your neighbor?'

'Susanta Gowswami. It is the spelling. Actually it was difficult for me to pronounce at first but now I think I can pronounce properly.'

Manjulika sent a smiley. Alberto's message came again, 'Susanta says he finds many similarities between Italian and Indian culture and my neighbor Amanda feels same.'

'My friend also liked Italian boys a lot. I also have two Italian friends of Facebook. I also think emotional level of us are matched somewhere.'

'You have two more friends from here?'

'Yes'

'From which places?'

'One from Venice and one from Florence.'

'Okay.'

'You visited those places?'

'Sure both places many times. I have friends also from both places.'

'I want to visit Italy once and Venice for sure.'

'Always welcome dear. If you come here I shall guide you everywhere.'

Manjulika did not understand what to reply to a friend with whom she had become friend that day. She sent a smiley.

Smiley with love sign came from another side. Manjulika asked, 'So who are in your family?'

'Me and my mother live together. My father lives at other place as my mother and father are separated. Sometimes I visit my father to stay with him.'

'Oh okay.' Manjulika replied not finding any other reply. Message came from other side, 'Who are in your family?'

'My parents, my elder sister and me.'

'Oh small nuclear family. Somewhere I heard there are many joint families in India.'

'Yes in old days and now many families are nuclear, may be more families are nuclear.'

'Okay.' Message came again, 'May I ask you one question if you don't mind.'

'At first you ask then I can understand.' Manjulika replied thinking Alberto would ask her number.

A smiley came from Alberto's side then another message came, 'I heard caste is a big problem in your country.'

Manjulika smiled little and said, 'Not caste, actually class and it is a problem and I think it is everywhere in this world. In basis of class castes were created in long past and now many generations from so-called low castes are richer than so-called higher caste but they are taking advantage from government and many people from higher-class are suffering.' Manjulika wrote again, 'In time of marriage some people think to match caste, but so-called low caste can change their surname then they will not feel problem, why they don't? To take advantage from government?'

'Understand.'

'I think within ten years all will do love-marriage here also. Matrimonial site will be used only as dating app and that time caste will also not be a problem. Though people fall in love also doing calculation sometimes I think.'

A smiley came from other side.

Manjulika saw that and heard her mother Rita's voice, 'Have you become totally mad or what Madhu?'

Manjulika guessed what discussion was happening between her mother and elder sister. Manjulika wrote Alberto, 'Okay I have to leave now.'

'Why?'

'I have some works.'

'Okay. Very nice to talk with you. Hope to chat with you soon.'

'Hope so. Okay bye.'

'Bye dear.'

Manjulika kept her mobile on bed and went to Madhulika's room. She thought she had guessed right about which discussion was happening in that room. She entered the room and found Madhulika was sitting on bed and Rita was standing in front of her. Both looked at Manjulika. Then Rita looked at Madhulika. Madhulika said, 'Maa why are you behaving like this?'

'Why are you behaving like this? Have you become mad or what?'

'Maa why don't you understand?'

Manjulika dragged a chair and sat on that. Rita said, 'What should I understand? What should I understand? Is there anything to understand?'

'Maa…'

'Listen Madhu now we should discuss about it seriously.'

'I am talking seriously.'

Rita glared at Madhulika. Madhulika took a pause and said, 'Maa please try to understand. We are different from others or vice-versa others are different from us.'

'Different? It is ridiculous thinking.'

'Maa try to understand Didi…' Manjulika said.

Rita glared at Manjulika and said, 'You keep quiet.'

Manjulika kept quiet. Madhulika said, 'Maa I really want to stay with a girl. She is my very good friend. Good friend can be good life partner.'

'Very good that you love your friend but don't want to make her your life partner.'

'Why not Maa?'

Rita glared at Madhulika once again. After a pin-drop silence Madhulika said, 'Maa you always said me the relation of love should be happened between two minds. If it is about mental bonding at first then the bonding can be happened within two minds, gender does not matter there.'

Rita looked at Madhulika for three seconds and said, 'Have you become really mad?'

'Maa I really like my friend. I thought a lot. I don't feel any interest about any boy. They can be brother or more than that friends only.'

'Madhu you have become really mad? And who is this friend? Her parents do not tell her anything?'

'I shall disclose her name after you and Baba agree for it and her father has died and mother also tells like you, to break the relation.'

'Good at least her mother has some intelligence.'

'Maa listen I really want to stay whole life with her.'

'Do you think about our social status?'

'She is belonging from my status. I am doctor and she is a school teacher just like you. Her father was an engineer.'

'Madhu.' Rita shouted.

'Yes Maa where is the problem? If I wanted to marry a boy from my status then was there any problem?'

'Madhu…'

'Maa see gender does not matter. See Manjulika has two close friends. Sobha and Kajal. Do you have any problem about her friendship with Kajal? After all she is third-gender.'

'So what? Is Manju marrying her?'

Manjulika giggled. Rita said, 'And who says I don't have any problem? I always felt little uneasiness about her but okay she is just friend.'

'Maa you always had problem about Kajal?' Manjulika asked looking at her mother. Rita looked at her with a disturbed expression. Madhulika said, 'Maa please try to understand. Please understand my situation. If you don't understand you read some books on it.'

'I don't have any need to read any book. I never thought my daughter can say it. I don't know how will your Baba react when he will hear.'

'Maa you please understand. If you don't understand who will make Baba understand.' Madhulika said.

Rita looked at Madhulika for few seconds then went near Madhulika and kept a hand on her shoulder and said, 'Madhu…, please try to understand.'

Madhulika held hand of Rita and said, 'Maa please you try to understand.' Rita looked at Madhulika for few seconds and left the room. Madhulika wanted to make a female her life partner. She was in a relation with her school friend Soma. She wanted to spend future life doing live in with her. Madhulika kept quiet few seconds. Manjulika went near her and sat beside her. Madhulika kept quiet few seconds more and looked at Manjulika and said, 'Manju…'

Manjulika looked at Madhulika. Madhulika kept quiet few seconds and asked, 'Manju if I shall settle in USA with Soma, will you be able to take care of Maa and Baba alone?' Madhulika said again, 'I shall send some money regularly.'

Manjulika smiled little then went little closer to Madhulika and kept a hand on Madhulika's hand, 'Didi?'

'Really now I have to think about it seriously. I am asking you seriously.'

Manjulika took a pause and said, 'Didi I will take care of them sure. You will send money or not I shall take total care and our parents don't need our money at-least. But I shall take other cares. If I was only one child then?' Madhulika smiled. Manjulika asked, 'But Didi are you sure?'

'Yes Manju. Now I have to think about it seriously. Soma also wants to settle in life. I don't want to wait more.'

'I understand.'

'Then seriously will you take care of Maa and Baba? I shall send money regularly. Sometimes I can visit. Too much pressure will be on you and specially after your marriage. And don't know where will you get married…, if you had any boyfriend then it was easier for me to take decision.'

Manjulika smiled little and said, 'Didi don't think too much. Life can't be planned like this. So what if today I had a long-distance relationship? Then we had to keep someone to take care of our parents. No one can tell future.'

'That is true.'

'Just don't think too much. You take your decision. I shall take care of Maa-Baba. You stay here or not does not matter. But try to convince Maa and Baba so you can start new life with Maa-Baba's blessings and ask Soma Di also to convince her mother.'

Madhulika smiled looking at Manjulika. Both hugged each-other.

2

∞

Manjulika and Sobha reached Kajal's house next of next of next Sunday after they had made the plan as because of Manjulika's colleague's wedding and then Kajal's fever plan for party of Manjulika, Sobha and Kajal had been cancelled two times. After reaching first floor Manjulika found the flower-vase and carpet were changed from last time. Manjulika had always found some changes in decoration of Kajal's house every time. Manjulika and Sobha reached Kajal's bedroom and found Kajal was sitting in front of laptop. She looked at Manjulika and Sobha and smiled and said, 'Come.'

Manjulika and Sobha went near her bed and shut down the laptop and went near bed and sat and they started chatting. After some time Kajal's dog Softy entered into room and sat on floor. Manjulika was afraid from dog, she kept a disturbed expression and shifted to corner of bed. After few seconds one ginger cat entered into room. Manjulika knew it was Kajal's elder brother's wife Moumita's cat. Manjulika liked cat a lot, she smiled little. Mango went near Softy and Softy ran away leaving the room and Mango followed Softy. Kajal said with a disturbed expression, 'Mango always disturbs Softy. Softy is far stronger than Mango but never beats her.'

'I saw many videos where cat disturbs dog but dog does not do anything.' Sobha said.

'Yes they also have some human like qualities.' Kajal said.

'It is not human like qualities. Generally human torture on weaker.' Sobha said.

'True.' Kajal said after few seconds, 'That day I was seeing a video where mother cat eating own kittens.'

'I also saw. Natures of animals also differ from each-other like human.' Sobha said.

'I also saw and I heard about one this kind of cat from my grandmother also.' Manjulika said.

'Yes many things were in society from many days, now those things are public.' Sobha said.

'Right.' Kajal said as Manjulika found one message from her neighbour friend Rahul. Manjulika read the message and smiled little and looked at Sobha and Kajal and said, 'Rahul is throwing a party in next Tuesday because he has gotten a t-shirt which he was searching for a long time. He has invited me and Manju Didi. He is really crazy.'

Kajal gave a smile. Sobha gave a pale smile after few seconds and said, 'Some people just try to find ways to spend money and I celebrated my birthday only one time in my life and memory of that birthday is also not very clear because I was five years old that time.'

Manjulika and Kajal exchanged an embarrassed expression. Manjulika was belonging from a so-called high-middle class family and Kajal from a higher class family and Sobha from lower-middle class family. Many times Sobha had discussed about economical difficulties of her family with Manjulika and Kajal. Kajal said, 'And I think if I was born in a poor family but being female it could be better.'

Sobha smiled and said, 'And I think opposite, if being third-gender I was born in a rich family it could be better.'

Manjulika felt helpless, she could not find any problem to share.

Kajal said, 'But we are exception. People can say female or male child come does not matter but no one will ever say male, female or third gender will come does not matter.'

'One of my relative has a differently abled child and she was telling if she had child of third-gender it could be better, may be parents of conjoined twins also think same.' Manjulika said.

'Right.' Sobha said.

Kajal smiled little.

Softy entered into room once again and Mango after that and then both left. Kajal glared looking at the door and said, 'Constantly Mango is disturbing Softy. One day I got into a fight also with Boudi about it.'

'How is your relation between you and Moumita Boudi now?' Manjulika asked. Moumita was Kajal's Boudi's name.

'Getting worse day by day, my brother is also changing.' Kajal took a pause and said again, 'Anyway I understand after marriage life partner is more important.'

'Good you understand.' Manjulika said.

Kajal smiled little and said, 'But you know that day I heard Boudi was telling one of her friend, she has gotten sister-in-law and brother-in-law together. I understood I think myself a female but many people remember my identity who know about it.'

'Forget it. You look like more female that many females. What is inside your dress does not matter.' Sobha said.

'Right.' Manjulika said.

Kajal smiled little and said, 'I remember when first time I disclose my identity to both of you I was really scared you would continue friendship or not but I did not want to hide it.'

'But till we are friends.' Sobha said.

Kajal smiled and said, 'You know why I keep Softy with me?'

Manjulika and Sobha looked at her. Kajal said, 'Not only because I love dog but I think Softy will not know about identity ever and will love me always not knowing my identity.'

Manjulika felt shaken.

'Sometimes I think if I was not born in an economically stable family what life I was living with my identity.' Kajal said.

'Leave it. How is going your work in Kaku's business?' Sobha asked looking at Kajal.

'Going fine. How is going your interviews?'

'Yes I am giving interviews, let's see.' Sobha said and smiled little and said again, 'Tanmoy has gotten a good job. After I shall get we are planning to marry.'

Manjulika and Kajal exchanged a smile.

'Hey Manjulika, say one thing? How is Alberto? I saw him to give you very romantic comment.'

Manjulika smiled little. Kajal said, 'I think he likes you.'

Manjulika smiled more and said, 'Don't know why I agreed to give him my number after asking for twice and he wants to send me a gift and I agreed.'

'What? Wow!' Sobha said and smiled looking at Kajal.

'Sometimes he gives me hints as he wants a special relation with me but for me we are just friends and after all he is Italian.'

'Really he is foreigner but all boys who chase you as I know I find best among them.' Sobha said.

'No one knows who is written in whose destiny.' Kajal said.

Manjulika smiled.

'Anyway let's see, I also took six months to understand I should tell yes or not to Tanmoy.' Sobha said.

Manjulika gave a shy smile.

After talking some time more and doing lunch Manjulika and Sobha left Kajal's house. After reaching house Manjulika came to know her father had come to know about Madhulika's relationship status. Manjulika talked with her mother for some time and her mother asked Manjulika to convince Madhulika to leave the relation but Manjulika did not agree. Manjulika entered into her room and Alberto's call came after some time, Manjulika felt thrilled and received after three rings, 'Hello!'

'Hello dear, how are you?'

Manjulika took a pause and said, 'Actually today I have a mixed day.'

'How?'

'I enjoyed a lot with my friend Sobha and Kajal at Kajal's house.'

'Wow!'

'But after coming at home I have to come to know my father has come to know about my Didi wants to stay whole life with a girl.'

'Oh…'

'Yes!'

'I think it is good, truth should come out as first as possible!'

Manjulika kept quiet few seconds and said, 'Yes but you know I thought he would be angry, he would be furious, he would shout for long time on Didi but he is keeping quiet. I am little tense for that.'

'Sometimes people does not react how we think. Actually there no guarantee of anything in life. You know the relation between my father and mother is becoming better day by day.'

'Very good.' Manjulika replied and continued talking with Alberto for half-an-hour more and then started dreaming about joining her most favourite reality show Super Boss.

3

Manjulika took her bag and went near her mother's room. She found her mother was sitting on a chair in front of T.V. but T.V. was not on. Manjulika asked, 'Maa will not you go to school today?'

'No.' reply came after few seconds. Manjulika kept quiet for a second and looked at Madhulika's room and guessed Madhulika was not there. Manjulika looked around and did not find her father anywhere. Rita had become absent from work very rare. Manjulika found Mithu was cleaning floor. Manjulika asked, 'Mithu Mashi where is Didi?'

'She has left for hospital.'

'And Baba?'

'He has also left for work.'

Manjulika looked at her mother for few seconds and said, 'Maa I am going to work.'

Rita looked at Manjulika once then smiled little and said, 'Yes okay, go carefully, bye.'

Manjulika smiled and said, 'Yes, you eat on time and take rest when you are at home today.'

Rita's face turned pale. Manjulika felt her mother was telling her, 'When my mental peace is gone, physical rest can't give me anything.'

Manjulika smiled little and left. After reaching office, after the security guard Manjulika met with Gautam. Manjulika tried to ignore him but Gautam smiled. Manjulika smiled back. 'Good morning!' Gautam said.

'Good morning!' Manjulika said and tried to leave the place. Gautam said, 'Why do you always avoid me Manjulika?'

It was a most common line Manjulika had heard from Gautam. Manjulika stopped, kept quiet few seconds and said, 'Then what should I do? I have work.'

'You also know if you talk with me for five minutes nothing will be happened.'

'But why do I talk with you without any reason?'

'Oh you can't talk with me without any reason?'

Manjulika kept quiet one second more and said, 'Not always.'

'Manjulika why you always behave with me like this?' Gautam asked and as Manjulika was going to reply, 'Bye.' Gautam asked, 'Anyway Manjulika who is Alberto?'

Manjulika felt a shock, within a second many questions came in her mind, how does Gautam know Alberto's name? Why does he want to know? Has he guessed anything between Alberto and her? And finally Manjulika thought why she is thinking if Gautam has guessed something, because there was nothing between Manjulika and Alberto in Manjulika's opinion. Then Manjulika guessed Gautam had come to know from Facebook. Manjulika looked at Gautam. Gautam smiled. Manjulika took a pause to think what to answer and said, 'He is my Facebook friend.' Manjulika took a pause once again and said, 'I think you also know that but why?'

'His comment is very different in your profile.'

'Why are you bothering?'

Gautam gave a puzzled smile then said, 'Can't I ask? Why do you talk with me like this always?'

'How am I talking? I just ask why are you bothering?'

Gautam smiled. Manjulika said, 'Okay bye.' Gautam smiled more and said, 'Bye.' Manjulika smiled little forcefully and left. As she was walking towards her table she found something covered with gift wrap was kept on her table. Manjulika stopped almost instinctively and became puzzled. After a second she started to walk as trying to guess what was that and who had kept? Suddenly name of Alberto came in Manjulika's mind. Manjulika felt little thrilled thinking if somehow Alberto had come to know address of her office from Sobha or Kajal as they were in Manjulika's friend-list. Manjulika went near her table and her thinking was stopped seeing a gift card which was attached on gift, where was written, To Manjulika, from Gautam. Manjulika's mood was totally changed. Thrill was removed and she started to feel anger, tension, disturbance and noticed her collogue Nilima was looking at her. Manjulika had a good relation with her, Manjulika had shared problem of Gautam with her only in office.

Nilima stood up and came near Manjulika and said, 'I have seen it already.'

Manjulika kept quiet few seconds and said, 'Don't know why he is behaving like this. He is crossing all limits. I am really tense now. Many staffs are here. Some of them are very good to do gossiping.'

'Will you open it or will return?'

'Are you mad? It will be one kind of acceptance. I will return.'

'That's also right.'

'Should I call him and return or do I keep on his table?'

'Do I call him?'

'No I shall keep on his table.'

'Okay.' Manjulika went near Gautam's table and kept the gift on his table and came near her own table. Nilima said, 'Why he is doing this? Is it behavior of a gentleman?'

'I told him 'No' as politely as possible but his nature is forcing me to be rude with him.'

'He is coming.'

Manjulika looked in front and found Gautam was coming. Manjulika did not understand how to react. Gautam looked at his table and came near Manjulika. Nilima left the place and went near her table and sat on her chair. Gautam came near Manjulika and stood in front of her, Manjulika gave him a firm look.

'You have not opened the gift?' Gautam asked.

Manjulika kept quiet and said in mind, 'You can see that.' Gautam looked at her for few seconds and left and went near his table. Manjulika could not stop herself to look at Gautam's table once to see what he would do with the gift. She found Gautam sat on his chair and took out his mobile and started to do something with that. Nilima came near Manjulika once again and said, 'You forget about Gautam. You think about today's work.'

'Don't know how other collogues will react.'

'Don't think about it. These things happen.'

Manjulika kept quiet. Nilima left. After some time Manjulika left the office to go to a shopping mall to take opinion of people about an incident in Barasat, where a school girl had been raped. After leaving the office Manjulika found Gautam was standing in front of office. Manjulika was going to ignore him but he came near Manjulika. Manjulika looked at the camera person and said, 'You please go and sit in car. I am coming.'

'Okay.' Camera person replied and left.

Gautam looked at Manjulika and said, 'Why are you behaving like this Manjulika?'

Manjulika decided to be firm in a second and said, 'Why are you behaving like this?'

'How am I behaving?'

'How? Don't you know how? You are going so far. You have brought gift for me.'

'Yes I want to gift you. So what? Anything wrong is there?'

Manjulika took a pause and said, 'Listen Gautam we both work in same office. I don't want to make any bad relation with you but please stop all those things. Don't do these kinds of things again.'

'Manjulika…'

'Bye.' Manjulika said and left the place. Manjulika wanted to move back once to see what Gautam was doing but did not as she thought it could be a positive or even romantic sign for Gautam. Manjulika went near the car and sat in the car. Driver started the car, after some time camera person Turna said, 'The incident is very sad. Five boys raped one girl.'

'Really very bad.'

'I just want to kill those boys by my hand.'

'Many people want but then killer will be punished for taking law in own hand.'

Turna smiled little.

'Why some boys think they have right on girls? Rape or ordinary harassment same mentality.' Manjulika said and remembered about Gautam and visualized Gautam's face. Just after saying it Manjulika thought if Turna guessed something. Manjulika was not sure how many persons of office knew about that matter. Turna said, 'People say girls are harassed because of their dress but this girl was returning from school, was in school dress.'

'Those things are ridiculous. I was harassed in college everyday where I went wearing salwar-kamiz but I was never harassed in shopping-mall wearing jeans or knee length one piece or skirt.'

'Oh I have same experience.'

'Really?'

'Oh don't ask me. Throughout three years I was harassed.'

'Me too.'

'You know what happened once?'

'What?'

'One boy threatened to apply vermilion on me.'

'Oh it was common threat in our college too. Though no one threatened me but my friends faced it.'

'And you know that time what one boy from another belief said?'

Manjulika looked at Turna for a second then said, 'What? In your belief anyone can marry any girl just applying vermilion?'

'Yes. Oh ridiculous. Really a girl has to stay with a boy if he applies vermilion?'

'Of-course not.'

'Really.'

'You know one of my friend from another belief once asked me if from any boy's hand little vermillion is applied on a girl's forehead somehow then what the girl will do?'

Turna smiled. Manjulika said, 'I said not necessary they have to stay together. The girl and the boy and their families will decide.'

'Sure.'

'Anyway what happened after the boy threatened you to apply vermillion?'

'Honestly I was scared.'

'Natural.'

'I was feeling to run from there but controlled and before I could say anything luckily our professor came and he scolded the boy very much and told him if he would do this kind of behavior again then the sir would take him to principal's room.'

'Oh good. Was the boy from your department?'

'No I was from History and he was from Geography.'

Those subjects made Manjulika smiled, Turna looked at her and said, 'My friends also always made fun telling History and Geography.' Manjulika smiled more and the driver stopped the car because of signal. One beggar was coming near the car. 'Please don't give her anything. You almost always give.'

'They are poor. We should help them.' Manjulika said as the beggar came near the car. Turna was sitting that side. She started to look at the window of another side. Manjulika took out one note of ten rupees and gave to that beggar. The beggar took that touched her hand on forehead and left.

Turna glared at Manjulika and said, 'Ten rupees? Are you mad?'

'Ten rupees is nothing today. Though I give two or five rupees also sometimes.'

Turna smiled and said, 'Hey potato chips coming. Will you buy?'

'Oh yes, for a long time I have not eaten.' Manjulika said and the person came near the car with chips. Manjulika stopped her and bought one packet chips of her favourite company's favourite flavour. 'Oh you like to eat chips very much.' Turna said.

'I like almost every kind of junk food and fast food.' Manjulika said and opened the packet of chips and offered Turna.

Turna, 'No no. I have done lunch before outing from home.'

'Oh me too but I can eat chips any time. Take one at-least.' Manjulika said and the driver started the car after signal was changed.

Turna took one and said, 'Oh not washing hands we are eating.'

'Oh come on, many germs are going in our mouth and nose which we are not seeing.'

Turna smiled and put the chips in mouth.

'I have spent ten rupees for chips but the ten rupees which I have given to that person is a big thing.'

Turna smiled and said, 'I remember once you donated in an orphan house and posted. You did a nice thing actually.'

Manjulika smiled little, said, 'Thanks.' and put one chips in mouth. She said again after few seconds, 'Seeing that one of my Facebook friend said I was showing off but I think what's wrong if I want to post those photos? Some people will not give anyone anything just to do even show off, will show only own outing, tour, house, car's photo and does not matter why I gave, it helped them.'

'Don't know why some people want others to think like them or live life like them.'

'Really.' Manjulika replied and put one chips in mouth. After finishing that as she was going to put another, Turna said, 'Manjulika…'

'Yes.'

'Can you tell me why do those boys do it?'

Manjulika looked at Turna guessing Turna was talking about rapists of the case for which they were going to take public opinion.'

'Rape.' Turna said. Manjulika nodded.

'I think they can't feel what a girl goes through if she is raped.' Turna said and looked at driver once.

'Really…, they don't think if it will be happened with their mother or wife or sister then…'

'Some even don't care about female of their own family members also.'

'True and if someone does not have female family members then even he should not do it.'

'Yes right.'

After some more talking driver reached the shopping mall. Manjulika and Turna entered the mall started the shooting. Manjulika found two girls were eating ice-cream near an ice-cream parlour. Manjulika went near them, 'Hi!'

Both girls looked at Manjulika, one with a very confused and puzzled face and another girl with a smiling face. Manjulika smiled looking both of them and said, 'Hey this is Manjulika Basu from Today's World channel.'

'Yes I know you very well.' The girl who had looked at Manjulika with a smiling face said.

Manjulika smiled more, 'Okay what is your name?'

'Moupiya Baneerjee.'

'And you?' Manjulika asked looking at another girl.

The girl gave a shy and puzzled smile, waited for five seconds and replied, 'Debopriya Baneerjee.'

'We are not sisters, just our names are matched and surname is also same.' Moupiya said just as Manjulika was thinking if those girls were sisters. Manjulika smiled little and said, 'Okay.' and thought the girl Moupiya would be nice to ask question. Manjulika took a pause and made her expression and said, 'Okay I have a question for you.'

'Sure.' Moupiya replied.

'Do you know a very bad incident has recently happened in Barasat. Five boys have raped a girl and killed her doing too much torture?'

Moupriya's face turned pale and Debopriya's confused. Then Moupiya said, 'Yes I have seen the news. It is very very sad incident. Actually sad is a very small word for it.'

'Yes and our question is what should be the punishment for those boys?'

Moupiya took a pause and said, 'I think they should be hanged. No other punishment is suitable for them.' Moupiya said again, 'Actually I think they should get more painful death than hanging. They must be killed in same way how they killed the girl. Same brutal torture should be done once to all of them and they all should be killed in same way.'

'Okay then do you support punishment of death?' Manjulika asked.

'Sure.' Moupiya said again, 'Actually I want to tell something about it.'

'Sure.'

'I think punishment of death should never be vanished from anywhere. Even if the punishment is not given to anyone practically then even it should not be removed from law. Because if it will be in law then at-least some people will stop themselves from doing this kind of crime being scared if this punishment will be given in that person's case. Removing punishment of death from law means putting some innocent people's life in danger and making a way to save some criminal people from deserving punishment after killing someone.'

'Okay.' Manjulika said and looked at Debopriya and asked her, 'What is your opinion about this incident?' with a confused mind thinking if she was doing right or wrong asking that question to that girl. Debopriya kept quiet few seconds with puzzled face and said, 'Yes right, she is right. They must be punished.'

Manjulika moved back to camera and said, 'Okay Moupiya and Debopriya have shared their opinions with us.' Manjulika looked at Moupiya and Deborpiya and said, 'Thank you.' 'Its ok.' Moupiya replied. Debopriya gave a confused smile.

Manjulika left the place and went to food court. After reaching food court Manjulika found only two tables were empty. Manjulika looked at one table and found three boys and three girls were sitting at one table. Manjulika went near the table. Those boys and girls looked at her. Manjulika said, 'Hi I am Manjulika Basu from Today's World Channel.'

'Yes I know you very well.' One girl among them said.

Manjulika smiled little looking at her and then made her face serious and said, 'Okay I have a question for you.'

'Sure.' The girl replied with smile. Manjulika kept her serious face and held the mike in front of that girl and asked, 'What is your name? 'Kajal Sen.' The girl replied. For a second Manjulika's friend Kajal's face came in Manjulika's mind. Then she said, 'Okay do you know a very sad incident has happened in Barasat?'

All of six boys-girls' faces became puzzled. Manjulika said, 'A girl was raped and murdered by five boys.' For few seconds all of them kept quiet. Then Kajal said, 'Oh sure. Pathetic.'

'What punishment should be given to those boys according to you.?' Manjulika asked.

Kajal kept quiet for a second and said, 'Death punishment sure.'

'Okay.' Manjulika replied.

'Yes sure. Even if they just had raped the girl then even death punishment was perfect.' Kajal said.

Manjulika held the mike in front of a boy and asked, 'You name?'

'Sudip Ghosh.'

'What do you think?'

'I think they must get worst punishment than hanging. Hanging is a minimal punishment for them. They should be thrown to public and public should take care of them.' Sudip Ghosh said.

'That's not right. That's taking law in own hand.' One boy said from beside.

'Did they care about law?' Sudip Ghosh asked looking at that boy.

Manjulika asked looking at him, 'Your name?'

'Subhrojit Roy.' The boy replied. The boy said again, 'And I don't support giving someone to public at all. They should be punished according to law.'

'Which punishment is suitable according to you?' Manjulika asked looking at Subhrojit Roy.

Subhrojit took a pause and said, 'See I am against death punishment. I think death punishment should be vanished from everywhere. According to wrong deeds jail is only punishment and there a good teaching should be given to them so they can get a chance to lead a good person's life after punishment.'

'Oh really?' Kajal almost shouted. Manjulika held the mike in front of her face. Kajal said, 'They have no right to get second chance taking another person's life.'

'Why?' Subhrojit said. Manjulika held the mike in front of him. He said again, 'Hate bad works not a person who is doing bad work.' Subhrojit said.

'It is crime not bad work and for those kinds of criminals death is the only punishment. Who can take any woman's self-respect and dignity and any person's life, the person deserves only death punishment.' Kajal replied.

'Not at all. No one should be killed like this before time.' Subhrojit said.

'Time? If I person can kill someone before time then that person also should be killed.' Kajal said again, 'And it can set an example also for others.'

'Oh, then why this murder case happened? Before this also some murderers were hanged.' Subhrojit asked sarcastically.

'Oh, who knows more cases could be happened.' Kajal answered promptly.

Subhrojit smiled tauntingly and said, 'Death punishment is at all not acceptable.'

'Sure acceptable and punishment is not given to set example only. If someone do this kind of crime that person or those persons must be punished.' Kajal said. Manjulika was switching her mike between Kajal and Subhrojit. After a pause she asked looking at one other girl of this group holding her mike in front of her, 'Your name?'

The girl hesitated for few seconds and said, 'Komal Sharma.'

Manjulika thought any intelligent answer is not coming from her. She asked, 'What is your opinion about this matter?'

Komal Sharma showed hesitation few seconds and said, 'If a person does mistakes the person must be punished.'

Manjulika felt asking her any other question would not be good. She held the mike in front of one other girl among three and asked, 'Your name?'

'Soma Som.'

Manjulika felt little surprised and hid her expression and remembered her Didi's girlfriend Soma once and asked, 'What is your opinion about this matter?'

'I think death punishment is too much. In this kind of case they must get life-time prison though life-time means life-time not fourteen years and in murder and rape both cases this rule should be applicable.' Soma said.

'Yeah that's okay. Subhrojit said.

Manjulika held the mike in front one other boy and asked, 'Your name?'

'Rajat Ghosh.'

'Okay what is your opinion about this matter?' Manjulika asked.

'I think they must get death punishment only, rape or murder whatever.' Rajat said again, 'And I think every murderer should get death punishment in same way how the person kills someone.'

'Exactly.' Kajal said.

'That's at all not right. Court, country and society no one has right to take anyone's life.' Subhrojit said.

'Oh you can't see the matter like this. It's punishment according to seriousness of their crime. No one is asking to hang any thief. I think to hate crime and criminals both sometimes. If no one does crime then crime will be a matter only in this world which would not be happened in reality. Everything can't be forgiven.' Kajal said.

'Oh common we are humans not animals. So eye for eye or life for life is not for us.' Subhrojit said.

'Of course it's right. Those people who can take other's life they are not human from inside, only biological body of someone does not make someone human, actually even many animals don't kill other animals like this. They are worse than animals. They must get death punishment otherwise if they come out from jail that can be a threat for society and specially for murdered person's family.' Kajal said. Manjulika said, 'Okay thank you everyone.' and moved back to camera and said, 'See everyone what today's generation think about this incident.' Manjulika went to other table where two boys and girls were sitting. Manjulika took their opinions and went on road and asked the question to some more people and finishing the shoot she reached home two hours later. After washing hands and face and changing dress Manjulika lied down with mobile and opened her Facebook profile and saw three new friend requests and two messages and twenty-three notifications came. Manjulika looked at notifications once and saw three friend requests and did not find any profile interesting. Manjulika opened messages and found one message from her friend, Abhishek Basu, 'Hi how r u?'

Manjulika found he was not online. She wrote, 'Fine and u.' and saw next message, it was from her friend Sunil from Delhi, 'Hi how r u'

Manjulika saw he was not online, she replied, 'Hi I am fine & u? How is Babita Bhabhi and Gaurav and Ashu?' and heard knock on the door. Manjulika guessed Mithu came as only she always knocked door before entering, Manjulika said, 'Come!'

Mithu entered and said, 'One currier has come in your name. Your Didi was at home. She took and gave me to give you.'

Manjulika suppressed a smile and said, 'Okay keep on bed.' Mithu kept the gift on bed and left. Manjulika took the packet in hand and saw Alberto's name on it. Manjulika smiled and found Alberto was calling on her mobile. She smiled more and received after three rings, 'Hello!'

'Hello dear! What are you doing?'

'I just have returned from work and you?'

'Oh I am in office.'

'Yes there is afternoon, here is everning.'

'Yes, anyway as I said I have sent the gift, have you received?'

'Yes just today has come. It is with me now.'

'Oh nice. Please open.'

'Okay.' Manjulika said and smiled and opened the gift rap and found an envelope was there. She tried to hide her emotion from her voice and said, 'It's an envelope.'

'Open please.'

'Okay.' Manjulika said and opened the envelope of pink colour and found a handmade card was there. Two red heart shapes were attached with each-other and some small hearts were drawn all over the card on pink paper. Manjulika felt thrilled and heard Alberto's voice, 'Hi dear have you opened?'

'Yes, nice card!' Manjulika said and opened the page of inside.

'Will you read the page of inside?'

‘Okay!’ Manjulika said to Alberto and said in mind, ‘I am eagerly waiting to do it.’ and read, ‘Dearest Manjulika, you are the person in my life for whom I care most in this outside world from my family. I didn’t think about relationship, emotional bonding, love too much ever in my life. I opened Facebook account after my friend had insisted and after that some close friends and relatives were in my Facebook and somehow friend-list started to get increased and don’t know when a friend who lives most far from me became closest to my heart and today I want to ask a question to you. Will you make me feel the luckiest person of whole world giving me a chance to share my life with you?’

Manjulika wiped her tears, kept quiet few seconds and said, ‘Hello!’

‘Hello dear!’

Manjulika could not say anything.

‘Hello!’ voice came from Alberto’s side.

Manjulika kept quiet few seconds more and said, ‘Your message has touched my heart.’

‘Really? My pleasure.’

After a silence Alberto’s voice came again, ‘Though I know I can’t write well.’

Manjulika smiled. Alberto’s voice came, ‘I just wrote whatever came in my mind.’

‘That is the best thing you have written.’

‘I am at all not good in artistic field. Honestly I wanted to draw a rose with it but after wasting ten papers, eleventh time I drew two big size heart-shape and some small hearts.’

Manjulika smiled and said, ‘The card is very nice.’

‘I saw your painting on Facebook, my card is just nothing comparing to that.’

'It was really cute.'

'Thanks.'

After a silence Alberto's voice came, 'Dear!'

'Yes!' Manjulika said and felt thrilled.

'I like you. If you will come in my life it will be my pleasure. I will feel the luckiest person in whole world.'

Manjulika kept quiet. Alberto's voice came, 'Dear please say something!'

Manjulika took a pause and said, 'Alberto, you are my very good friend but…, you can understand… there is no match between us practically.'

'If our minds match then nothing matters.'

'Alberto…, you also know very well the difference between us.' Manjulika said again, 'Hearing about your family and life style I feel we both are belonging from same economical status after being from different countries…, and surprisingly we are belonging from same belief, actually I never thought I would ever a get friend from same belief but western country but our culture, citizenship…, you know very well…'

'See by chance we are belonging from same belief so I don't propose you.'

'I know that.'

After a pause reply came, 'Hey are you thinking from western country finding girl from same belief is difficult for me so I am proposing you? If you think that…'

'No no not at all.'

After some time Alberto's voice came, 'Manjulika…'

'Yes.'

'See for me relations matter. Though I never cared for emotions a lot ever in my life but after meeting with you don't know what happened…'

Manjulika smiled.

'Again Alberto's voice came, 'Manjulika culture, life style those are all small matters, and if we will marry it will be mixing of cultures and life styles.'

After a pause Manjulika said, 'Yes mixing of culture is nice.'

'Right.'

'But…'

'But what dear?'

'There are many things to think.'

'I don't need. I am sure you are the person with whom I want to spend my whole life.'

Manjulika took a pause again and said, 'Alberto I need time to think.'

After some time Alberto's voice came, 'Okay dear, but we can stay good friends like before?'

'Sure and always.' Manjulika said and heard knock on the door. She pressed mute button and said, 'Come in.' Mithu entered with Aloo Chop and placed on bed-side table and left. Manjulika clicked unmute option.

'Hello what happened?' Alberto's voice came.

'My maid came to give supper.'

'Oh what is the item?'

'Aloo Chop.'

'Oh one kind of Indian potato fry right? With coating of batter, like hash-brown?'

'Yes, you remember?'

'I remember everything about you and your culture.'

Manjulika smiled and asked, 'So what had you in lunch?'

'Macaroni and Tiramisu.'

'Wow Tiramisu. I just like it. I tried it twice at home but it was not as tasty as Italian restaurant.'

'Hope one day you will come at my home and my mother will make you learn to make it and I shall taste Tiramisu which will be made by you and I think it will be tastier than restaurant as I find my mother's Tiramisu is tastier than restaurant.'

Manjulika smiled and asked to avoid the topic, 'Anyway how is going your business?'

'It is going smooth.' Alberto's reply came. Manjulika and Alberto continued talking for a long time.

4

∞

Manjulika was standing beside the chair where her father was sitting. Manjulika said, 'Baba!' Her father Animesh kept quiet. 'Baba!' Her father did not reply. She said again, 'Baba!'

'What?' Her father replied.

Manjulika did not expect a reply just after three times, so she got puzzled to reply. After a pause she said, 'Baba..., Baba please try to understand Didi.' It was first time Manjulika was trying to make Animesh understand about Madhulika. Before that only her mother had tried to do it as Rita had agreed with Madhulika's decision very reluctantly before some days and said she did not have any problem if Animesh would agree. Manjulika did not understand what to say next. Manjulika had felt a hesitation from starting but as her mother Rita and elder sister Madhulika had insisted her a lot to talk she had agreed. Manjulika took a pause and said, 'Baba please try to understand Didi!'

No reply came from her father. Manjulika waited some time and said, 'Baba everyone has own choice...'

'Babu go from where!' Manjulika's father called her Babu sometimes.

'Baba!'

'Go from where.'

'Baba!'

'I say go from where.' Animesh replied in firm voice.

Manjulika got puzzled for some time and stood keeping quiet and finally decided to leave. After she left that room, Rita called her from Madhulika's room, 'Manju!'

Manjulika looked at that room and went to that room. Manjulika kept quiet few seconds after she entered and finally told, 'Baba just did not talk to me. He does not want to discuss about this matter.'

Madhulika and Rita's faces got puzzled. After pin-drop silence for few seconds Madhulika said in a firm voice, 'I knew he would never agree.'

Manjulika and Rita both looked at Madhulika. Madhulika looked at Rita for few seconds and said, 'Whole life you tolerated his domination but I will not do that.'

Rita's face turned puzzled then little anger became visible with that. Madhulika said, 'Whole life, whole life he dominated we three but I am not going to tolerate any more.'

Rita and Manjulika exchanged a look. In Manjulika's family Manjulika had seen Animesh to control almost everything. Manjulika had seen Rita to make objection sometimes but most of the time she had seen Rita to agree for whatever Animesh had said. Manjulika had seen her elder sister to fight with her father from late teenage and she also had started that. Though Manjulika always found a good bonding among four family members of her family but she always found his father's dominating nature was a problem in her family. Madhulika said again, 'But now I am adult, not only adult and it is question about my life and I am not going to tolerate his domination any more.'

Manjulika and Rita kept quiet. Madhulika said again, 'Okay Maa I am getting late. I am ready, I am going to hospital. I am asking Mithu Mashi to close the door.'

Manjulika and Rita looked at Madhulika. Madhulika said, 'Okay bye Maa, bye Manju.'

'Bye.' Rita said.

'Bye.' Manjulika said.

Madhulika took her bag and left.

Manjulika and Rita kept quiet some time then Manjulika said, 'Maa please make Baba understand.'

No reply came from Rita's side. Manjulika looked at Rita once then started to look at the floor. After a silence in the room Rita said, 'Now I think it's my mistake.'

Manjulika looked at Rita. Rita said again, 'It's my mistake that my over pampering nature has spoiled both of you.'

Manjulika gave little smile and little false anger mixed expression. Rita looked at Manjulika and said, 'Now I think many times I stopped your father when he tried to be strict with you and your Didi, but I think he was right. Actually I should have been stricter.'

'You were also strict Maa. May be less than Baba.'

'Oh I was also strict? Almost always I fulfilled all your wishes even sometimes hiding your father. He almost always wanted to save money whole life.'

'Maa generally in other families it's different. Generally fathers pamper female children but our father is not like that and you fulfilled our demands and we never demand anything you can't fulfil.'

Rita kept a glum face some time then said, 'Now I think I should have thought about her personality before. I got many signs, many…'

Manjulika looked at her mother. Rita said again, 'Why I never told her anything when she did not wear saree in Saraswati Pujo…, why I never understood when she never wanted to keep her hair long even reaching college…, she never wore any imitation jewellery even I remember very well when she was in class seven one day she told me she does not want to wear that gold earrings which I had made her wear when she had been in class five.'

'Yes I also remember.'

'I felt little surprised and asked her why? She did not have any answer, she just said I don't want to wear. I felt little bad but I agreed…, still I keep that pair of earrings.' After a pause Rita said again, 'Even later she complained sometimes why I made whole in her ear.'

Manjulika kept quiet. After a long pause Rita said, 'Why I never thought there is something wrong in her personality? Why? Sometimes I felt bad when I saw after reaching teenage she is not changed but I thought she would change but never realized when she reached age of marriage but never changed…' Rita looked at Manjulika and said, 'But I never thought she would ask to stay whole life with a girl, I was thinking I would ask her to grow her hair because after some days she would get married.'

Manjulika smiled. Rita said, 'Why, why I never thought there is a reason behind her this kind of behaviour? Why?'

Both kept quiet some time then Manjulika said, 'Maa you could not do anything. It is her personality.'

Rita kept some time and asked, 'From when do you know?'

'When she understood that time even my period was not started so I was a child for her, after I reach class nine she told me.'

'Oh you knew from many years but did not tell me.'

'Actually I was not sure that she was sure or not about her decision. It took me two years to believe.'

'But after that two years had been passed and you did not tell me.'

'I thought Didi would tell when right time would come.'

'Right time? Right time for totally a wrong thing.'

'Maa…'

Rita stood up and went near the cricket bat which was kept beside the door in a corner. Manjulika got puzzled and stood up, went near her mother. Rita took the bat and said, ‘I will break it. I will break it. When on her eighth birthday she asked cricket set not a doll or kitchen set that time I should have understood.’ Rita tried to break the bat throwing on wall. Manjulika stopped her and said, ‘Maa don’t act like a child. Bat will not be broken, our wall will get a scratch.’ Manjulika took the bat and kept at place as she said, ‘Because of Didi I also got some experience to play cricket otherwise I don’t think I ever thought to play cricket ever.’ Rita kept an angry face. After a pause Manjulika said, ‘Okay Maa we both are getting late. I have to go to office. You also get ready and ask Baba to get ready. Manjulika was ready already. Rita said, ‘Okay go.’

‘Okay.’ Manjulika said and left room and went to her room. Using washroom Manjulika kept mobile in bag and left room and going near her parents’ room she found her mother was getting ready and her father was not there. Manjulika guessed he was in washroom. Manjulika told her mother, ‘Maa I am going.’

‘Okay.’

Manjulika asked Mithu to close the door and left home and booked a cab. Five minutes after she took the cab and a call from Alberto came. After Alberto had proposed Manjulika the relation was like friendship between Alberto and Manjulika for few days and after that it turned into unofficial courtship but Manjulika was not sure about the decision of marriage. Manjulika received, ‘Hello!’

‘Hello Dear!’

‘Yes tell!’

‘Where are you?’

‘I am going to office. On the way.’

‘Oh you are on road. I think I have done mistake to calculate time. Then will talk later.’

'No no I am in car. We can talk. I am little late today so I have taken car.'

'Oh late? And I thought almost one hour is left to go for your office.'

'Oh no no you calculated wrong.'

'Hope one day I shall not have to calculate. We will be together always sometimes in your country and sometimes in my country.'

Manjulika understood Alberto was talking about marriage. Manjulika smiled little and avoided the topic and said, 'Anyway what are you doing?'

'I am taking bed tea.'

'Oh.'

'Why are you late today?'

'Today my mother and Didi asked me to talk with Baba about Didi.'

'About Didi's relation with her partner?'

'Yes they wanted me to make agree Baba but Baba just did not want to talk with me about the matter.'

'Oh then what?'

'I don't know then what…, I really don't know. I asked Maa to make understand Baba but I think she already had tried enough.'

'You get married with me at first then I shall make him understand.'

'Nice joke.' Manjulika said and smiled.

'Anyway Manju your parents are already tense about your Didi's matter, how will they react if they will know we want to get married.'

'I also thought about it many times.' Manjulika said in mind and said to Alberto, 'Not necessary they have to think it.'

'Oh dear why say it and break my heart?'

'I just say the fact.'

'This fact breaks my heart.'

Manjulika smiled and said, 'Okay you say how is situation in your country?'

'Yes very critical situation.'

'Here also people are afraid. I think here also lockdown will be started soon.' Before some time, the disease Corona was introduced in the world.

'Oh there also?'

'Yes. Now people are becoming afraid of Corona here also day by day. Don't know when lockdown will be started. Let's see.'

'Oh.'

'Anyway how are your parents?'

'They are fine but tense about situation. I just have exchanged message with my Dad. My Mom is doing 'Puja' one kind of worship. I think you know.'

'Sure I know. Though I should not be surprised but I feel surprised hearing someone from western country doing 'Puja.'

'Understand.'

'Okay you take care for both of your parents and yourself.'

'Yes I wish they both were together then it could be easier.'

'Understand.' Manjulika said and saw her elder sister Madhulika's call was coming. Manjulika said, 'Hey Alberto my Didi is calling, will talk later.'

'Okay sure dear bye.'

'Bye.'

Manjulika cut the call and called Madhulika and found busy. She guessed Madhulika was trying her number. She waited and after some time Madhulika's call came. Manjulika received, 'Hello!'

'Hello Manju!'

'Yes Didi.'

'There is a very bad news.'

Manjulika got puzzled and tried to guess what can be but could not and asked, 'What?'

'Soma's mother has died this morning.'

'What?'

'Yes actually in early morning she got heart-attack and was taken to nearest hospital. Soma did not get time to inform me and before some time she has died.'

'Oh no.'

'Manju I am going to hospital.'

'Hospital means? Where Soma Di's mother was admitted? Are you going there?'

'Sure or what?'

'Yes, yes.'

'I have not reached our hospital. I change route and I am going there. They will take her mother at first to their house and some relatives will come there and after that they will take for cremation. If possible come after work at her home. I shall stay with her for some days now.'

'Sure I shall go to Soma Di's home directly after work.'

'Bye…'

'Bye.' Manjulika cut the call and reached her office and finishing shooting she went to Soma's flat. Soma, Madhulika and Soma's one neighbour and three relatives who had gone with Soma to cremation place and Soma's maid were there. After some time everyone left including Soma's maid except Manjulika and Madhulika. Madhulika locked the door after everyone left and three sat on sofa of sitting-room. They sat keeping quiet for some time and suddenly Soma broke into tears. For a second Manjulika got puzzled and looked Madhulika, Madhulika also looked at her. Then Madhulika went near Soma and kept a hand on her back. Soma looked at her. Madhulika hugged Soma and Soma broke into tears once again. Manjulika sat keeping quiet with a pale face. It was first time she was seeing any close person's mother's death. She had seen some relatives and neighbours' deaths but none of them were closer than Soma. After some time Manjulika also went near Soma and consoled her and Madhulika decided to stay with Soma till all religious rituals would be finished. Manjulika decided to bring some dresses for Madhulika before she would go to office next morning and left Soma's flat.

5

Manjulika, Madhulika and Soma were sitting on sofas of Soma's flat keeping quiet. All rituals after Soma's mother's death were finished that day. Ten minutes were passed after all relatives and neighbours of Soma had left from Soma's home. Manjulika said, 'Soma Didi why don't you come and stay with us for some days?'

Soma looked at Manjulika then at Madhulika. Madhulika said, 'Yes sure, now you come and stay at our home for some days.'

Soma kept quiet few seconds and said, 'At your home?'

'Yes Soma, how will you stay here alone in flat? For fifteen days you come.' Madhulika said.

'How long I stay at home. More than half of the day I stay outside for work and other time I sleep or watch movie or listen music, and my maid will also come, I can manage. Sometimes you visit..., sometimes I shall go at your home.'

'But not now, at least for one week you come yaar. Give leave to your maid.' Madhulika said.

Soma kept quiet. 'Yes Soma Didi you come and stay with us at least some days.' Soma did not reply. 'Yes Soma for at least one week you stay. Then later we can think.'

Manjulika thought later what will be happened in future? Will Manjulika and Madhulika's parents agree for Madhulika and Soma's relation? Where will Madhulika stay and where will Soma stay? Manjulika stopped thinking and said, 'Yes Soma Didi you come and stay for some days.'

Soma smiled little, took a pause and said, 'Okay.'

Manjulika and Madhulika smiled. Madhulika said, 'Do I help you in packing?'

'No no, no need, I shall manage.'

'Okay but we can help you.' Manjulika said.

Soma took a pause and said, 'Packing will be done but should I leave this flat like this?'

'What will you do if really any thief or robber will come? Will you be able to protect?' Madhulika asked. Soma smiled little.

Next day Soma came at Manjulika and Madhulika's home to stay. Rita consoled her a lot and next evening all sit together to see news channel. The news was announced for next twenty-one days no one would be able to go out from home because of Corona. After the news was finished Manjulika, Madhulika and Soma went to Madhulika's room. Soma sat on bed and after a pause she asked, 'How will I go home now?' as Manjulika sat on bed and Madhulika sat on a chair.

After a silence Madhulika said, 'No problem you stay here.'

Soma looked at Madhulika with a puzzled face. 'Yes why not?' Manjulika said. Soma kept quiet.

'I think it will be better, my parents will come to know about you more.' Madhulika said.

'Right.' Manjulika said.

Soma smiled little. Madhulika said after a pause, 'Okay but now we have to think how to buy grocery products, how to do other works of home.'

'I think just now we should go and buy some grocery items.' Manjulika said.

'Yes right, at least we can buy potato from there, always substitute of all vegetables.' Manjulika said.

‘Yes then, potato, onion, garlic, ginger and other items like biscuit, sugar, spices etc.’ Madhulika said.

‘Then me and Madhulika can go.’ Soma said.

‘Yes I think I should go and ask Maa to make final list, then we will go.’ Madhulika said.

‘Should I come?’ Manjulika asked.

‘No no, we will manage.’ Madhulika said.

‘Okay then I am going to my room.’ Manjulika said and stood up.

‘Okay.’ Madhulika said. Manjulika went to her room and found Alberto’s call, Manjulika received, ‘Hello!’

‘Hello dear, what are you doing?’

After a pause Manjulika said, ‘Don’t ask, here also effect of Corona has started in full form. Lockdown is started for twenty-one days. We have to do shopping of grocery items. My Didi’s friend Soma Di is staying with us. Though my profession and my Didi’s profession is different. Even in emergency we will go out.’

‘One emergency has come in my home. My mother has gotten heart-attack.’

Manjulika took a pause and said, ‘What?’

‘Yes.’

Manjulika took a pause and asked, ‘Is she in hospital?’

‘Yes, I am very worried. I can’t explain what I am feeling.’

Manjulika was struggling for words. After a silence from both sides Manjulika said, ‘Don’t worry she will be fine soon.’ Manjulika said and became worried and pray to God.

Alberto’s voice came, ‘I never felt so helpless in life. I never let her go out after Corona is started and now she is in hospital in time of Corona.’

Manjulika felt sad and helpless. Alberto said, ‘I am feeling helpless dear.’

‘Don’t worry, Aunty will be okay soon. I will pray to God.’

‘Please, please do it. I can’t remember ever I prayed or not to God in life but after this I am also praying.’

Manjulika smiled little. Alberto said, ‘I think your prayer will work more as you regular pray to God. I don’t know God will listen me or not.’

‘You just pray from your heart.’

‘Now I think I should have prayed to God regularly then today I don’t have to see this day.’

‘Now you don’t have to think about all those things. Take care of Aunty and take care of yourself.’

‘I have forgotten about myself, I just want my mother to be fine.’

‘No dear take care of yourself also otherwise who will take care of your mother.’

After a pause Alberto’s voice came again, ‘I never felt so helpless in life. I saw problems between my parents and their divorce in childhood, the loss in business two times but I never felt so helpless.’ Alberto said again, ‘Because my mother was always with me, she was strength of my life but today she is ill then to whom I talk for mental strength?’

Manjulika felt helpless. Alberto said, ‘Though I am feeling good after talking with you.’

Manjulika smiled and said, ‘You can talk to me whenever you want. Other than job time I can speak to you always.’

‘Thank you so much.’

‘Anyway what about Uncle?’

'Yes he regularly talks with me over phone and asks about my mother. In time of Corona he can't come.' Alberto said again, 'Manju…'

'Yes.'

'Once you said every bad thing has a good side.'

'Yes.'

'Today I feel that.'

'How?'

'Today I can understand actually how much my father loves my mother.'

Manjulika smiled little and said, 'Really?'

'Yes.'

'Very nice.'

After talking with Alberto for five minutes more Manjulika cut the call and went to kitchen and found Madhulika and Soma had bought grocery items for fifteen days. Manjulika said, 'Oh you have done a nice work.' Rita entered into kitchen and said, 'But don't buy anything more and specially in this kind of time of emergency, stock should be kept in shops for everyone.'

Manjulika, Madhulika and Soma looked at Rita then Soma smiled and said, 'You are right Kakima. We remembered that.'

'The Nayan Kaku also not giving many products to anyone. Ratri Boudi also went there and she was asking so many packets of spices but Nayan Kaku refused to give.' Madhulika said. Ratri was Manjulika and Madhulika's one cousin's brother's wife's name.

Manjulika smiled and said, 'Oh good.'

'Yes everyone should think about others of society, Ratri is always like this, selfish girl. I know her very well.' Rita said.

'Oh Maa has no son, but talking like mother-in-law for sister-in-law's daughter-in-law.' Manjulika said and giggled.

Madhulika and Soma smiled. Rita gave slight angry expression with little smile. Mithu entered into kitchen and said, 'Okay you all go. I shall keep everything at right places.'

'Okay.' Madhulika said and Madhulika and Soma left kitchen, Manjulika and Rita also left then. Manjulika went to her bedroom, sat on her bed, kept quiet few seconds and started to pray to God for Alberto's mother.

6

Manjulika was sitting in front of window with a cup of coffee. She took a sip. It was winter of twenty-twenty. Corona had spread in whole country. Manjulika and her elder sister were going for job. Soma was staying at home with their parents whole day. She had not gone back to her home after she had come to Manjulika parent's house after her mother's death. Manjulika's one classmate from school, one classmate's husband from college, two relatives, one neighbor and some known of known people had died from Corona. Alberto's mother's health was okay but his father had suffered from Corona and became okay. Manjulika's personality was changed in last some months. She had understood many mistakes of life after Corona. Manjulika had a leave that day. She took another sip of coffee and opened Facebook profile and found her collogue Gautam's father had died for Corona. Gautam had not disturbed Manjulika after the day she had rejected his gifts and after that there was relation of hi-hello between them. Manjulika felt little bad and decided to give a cry sign and wrote according to her, 'Feeling very sad' then checking some more messages, notifications and friend requests Manjulika left the room for balcony. As she was passing her parents' room she found Soma was sitting with her mother. Manjulika heard Soma to say, 'After coming here I have gotten a mother.' Manjulika stopped going little far from the door so Rita and Soma can't see her but she could hear their conversation. After few seconds Rita's voice came, 'I also have a new daughter. Sometimes I think in lockdown period Madhu and Manju both are going out and I am not going to school and this time you are here so I am not feeling alone.'

After some time Soma's voice came, 'But Kakima I think I am disturbing you all.'

'No, no why are you thinking like this? Not at all. Even sometimes Madhu's father also says you are at home so we are not feeling alone.'

'I also think if I was at my home then I became totally alone and my mother's memory is in whole flat and if I was alone there…' After Soma's voice, sound of Soma's crying came.

'Soma…, Soma…', Rita's voice came. Manjulika heard Soma to cry constantly. Manjulika went near the door of her parents' room and saw Rita hugged Soma. Soma was crying hugging Rita. Rita looked at Manjulika once. Manjulika went near the bed and sat. Soma looked at her once and hugged Rita tighter and started to cry more. Rita passed hand on Soma's back. After crying some time more Soma left Rita and wiped her tears. Soma looked at Manjulika and said, 'Now she is my mother also.'

Manjulika smiled and thought does Soma told it to please her mother and to make her agree for Madhulika and Soma's relation? Manjulika stopped thinking and said, 'So now I have to fight for my mother with Didis. Me and Didi always have a fight that whom Maa loves more.'

Soma smiled and said, 'Sometimes I also think if I had a sister or brother could they reduce my pain?'

'Who have no sibling they may think like that. My brother rare took any responsibility of my parents after settling in USA. I always took and gave share of fifty percent property.' Rita said. Manjulika smiled. Soma wiped her tears once again and smiled little.

After a silence Soma asked looking at Manjulika, 'Anyway Manjulika how is your classmate's mother who was suffering from Corona?'

'Yes luckily she is fine now but my classmate from school has died I forgot to tell.'

'Oh sad.' Soma said.

'My one friend was telling she was only child but I think that does not matter. Parents feel equal pain if they lose a child among two or three.'

'Really Corona is destroying many lives, don't know how her parents are managing now.' Rita said with a very sad face.

Manjulika looked at Soma and said, 'You know after my neighbour Samir Kaku has died…'

'Yes.' Soma replied.

'I heard my Jethima to say his wife has no child then how will she live whole life then child is a time-pass only or a time-pass also?' Manjulika said.

'Right.' Soma said.

'Not that but it could be easier for her to bear the pain.' Rita said. Manjulika and Soma looked at Rita. Rita said again, 'But everyone finds own way to live.'

'Yes everyone does not have to have a child. Those people who marry in same gender don't have child. Sometimes they adopt.' Manjulika said.

Soma's face became puzzled.

Rita kept quiet some time and said, 'I think your Didi is also going to do it. She will give us an adopted grandchild.'

Manjulika and Soma looked at each-other. Then Manjulika said, 'Maa but Didi will be happy if Baba and you will agree at first.'

'What option is left for us?' Rita kept quiet some time and said.

'Didi will be happy if you and Baba will agree happily.' Manjulika said. Rita kept quiet. After few seconds Manjulika said almost suddenly, 'Maa Soma Didi is that girl.'

Soma looked at Manjulika with surprised and scared expression. Rita looked at Manjulika with a surprised expression for a second then at Soma. Then Rita started to look at the bedcover. Manjulika and Soma looked at each-other with nervous faces. After some time Rita looked at Manjulika and said, 'So keeping her here was a plan?'

'No, no Maa, not at all. She came for some days, we never had plan to keep her here but Corona was started so…, and Soma Didi did not want to come…'

Rita smiled little. After silence of some time in the room Rita said, 'You both go from here, now.'

'Maa..'

'I don't want to talk now, just leave me alone for some time.'

Manjulika and Soma looked at each-other then Soma said, 'Let's go.' and left the bed.

Manjulika kept a hesitated face, Rita glared at her, Manjulika left the bed. Manjulika and Soma looked at each-other coming out from room, Manjulika said, 'Come with me in balcony.'

Soma nodded after one second.

Manjulika and Soma both went to balcony. They took two chairs and sat. 'Why have you told it suddenly?' Soma asked looking at Manjulika.

Manjulika took a pause and said, 'Suddenly I thought those things should be said suddenly.'

'Why?'

'Then shocking impact will be less according to me.'

'Really?'

'Yes.'

'But she is thinking taking time.'

'But I think she will agree soon.' Manjulika said again, 'You know after you have come the atmosphere of our home has become little normal. Baba is also talking with everyone very normally.'

Soma smiled little and pointed at the next door of neighbour and said, 'See that Kakima is again wasting food.'

Manjulika looked at that house and said, 'Really does not know why she throws food in drain always, at least if she gives in the side of road then cats and dogs can eat. Really very bad nature, I think she has sadistic disorder, she can't see anyone happy. Some people are like that, jealous from cat and dog also.'

'May be, whatever wasting food is very bad.'

Manjulika kept quiet few seconds and said, 'Though with this thought I don't agree. Many people say it.'

Soma looked at Manjulika with puzzled face. Manjulika said, 'Actually people say don't waste food, but for me it's a wrong concept. The thinking should be don't waste ration.'

'What is the difference?'

'Difference is don't waste food means, don't waste cooked food. If people think let's cook whatever we want, we will not waste, we will eat everything. But after food is cooked does not matter we will eat or throw. Too much eating than need is a bad thing for health and it is also one kind of wasting. So people should think we should not cook too much. If we cook how much we want then ration will be kept in our kitchen and then we will go to market again not so early to buy ration and ration will be stored more and it will be good for all society as an asset specially in the time of Corona.'

Soma took a pause and said, 'Wow never thought in this way.'

Manjulika smiled little. Soma said, 'But wasting food is not good. It seems very bad throwing food in garbage pot or in street.'

'Yeah that's right.'

After some time keeping quiet Soma asked, 'Hey how is Sumita?'

Manjulika looked at Soma, took a pause and asked, 'Sumita? My friend?'

'Yes.'

'Yes she was in depression and after Corona she is more depressed. For a long time she was trying for job.'

'Is she consulting astrologer and tarot card reader still?'

'Sure but now online.'

'Okay.'

'I consulted also before getting job, five astrologers and two-three tarot card readers. Still I am in contact with three astrologers and two tarot card readers among them.'

'Really?' After a pause Soma said, 'Sometimes I think if I consulted any astrologer before my mother's death who knows if she could survive. My mother believed a lot but after she became ill she could not visit our family astrologer. She asked me once but I did not go and now I feel very guilty.'

Manjulika's face turned pale, she took a pause and said, 'Who knows. I don't understand still if they can change anything or not and if can then how much, but they can predict sure.'

'But prediction matching can be con-incidence. Some people tell if they tell many things then something will be matched.'

'Soma Di how much correct astrology is, it does not depend on how many percent predictions are correct, you have to see those things which are matched that can be co-incidence or not.'

Soma gave a puzzled look.

'Means if someone predict someone will die within her or his sixty to sixty-five years of age and if the person by-chance dies in that period which is early-death in today's life that also can be co-incidence but I saw someone to predict death year and it was January month.'

'Oh really?'

'Yes the mentioned year was correct.'

'Very strange.'

'My mother also made my horoscope and Didi's horoscope and many things are matched.'

'Oh.' Soma took a pause and asked, 'It was also written she would be engaged with a girl?'

Manjulika took a pause, smiled little and said, 'Actually you know there is not written very much about Didi's married life. I think either astrologer did not understand, as relation in same gender was not so famous that time or he understood and wanted to avoid.'

'Oh…' Soma asked after some time, 'How is tarot card reading experience?'

'Amazing, I met three tarot card readers, with two of them my experience is very good.'

'Oh, I went to one astrologer once with my mother.'

'Your family astrologer?'

'Yes.'

'That gentleman predicted anything about you?'

'Not man, she is female.'

'Oh.'

'And surprisingly her many predictions came true and past also matched.'

'Oh.'

'But I did not consult before my mother's death, in the time of illness. Though her prediction about death time is almost matched.'

'Really?'

'Yes approx. So I think it was destiny.'

'May be.'

'But sometimes I also think how those predictions come true and feel surprised. How anyone can tell about future.'

'I think everything is pre-decided.' Manjulika said again, 'Actually I knew about many persons who learn astrology or palmistry just for interest and they are successful in other fields of career. They don't take money but their predictions became so accurate even in exceptional situation.'

'Really, you saw any prediction like this?'

'Actually I heard, one girl had flight ticket to go foreign after marriage but one person of local area who knew to see horoscope said I don't see any chance of going to foreign country. He was not professional and did not take money. He was teacher in high school.'

'Then…'

'After marriage the girl got panic attack thinking for five years she has to leave her parents. She started to cry a lot and finally the boy has to go alone.'

'Really? I can't believe this.'

'My mother said it. It happened in their neighbourhood.'

'Oh…'

'These kinds of predictions have made me believe astrology.'

'Recently now I am also developing a faith.' After some time Soma said again, 'Now any astrologer can predict when I shall die?'

Manjulika looked at Soma surprisingly with little puzzled and fear mixed expression. Soma looked at Manjulika and said, 'Yes after my mother's death now death has become a dream for me.'

Manjulika kept looking at Soma with more surprised expression. Manjulika saw smile and tears at same time on Soma's face. Soma said, 'Actually I think if I die I can meet my mother.'

Manjulika smiled very little. Soma said, 'Never thought one day death would be a dream for me.' Manjulika kept looking at Soma with little smile on her face.

Soma said, 'But you know sometimes I think if my mother will take rebirth.' Soma said again, 'You know surprisingly for first time I am getting interest for those beliefs who has no rebirth concept. If I believe in that thought then I don't have to be afraid for rebirth of my mother.'

Manjulika smiled little. Soma wiped her tears. Manjulika said, 'Did you ever think to communicate to Kakima through any medium?'

Soma smiled little and said, 'Do you really think it works?'

'I think sure there are other worlds beyond this world, which we can't understand properly.'

'May be.'

'Actually I started to realize it from few months after my Dida's death. I think after her death I started to get some spiritual feeling and of-course meeting with tarot card reader I have gotten some spiritual knowledge.'

'Oh…'

'Actually sometimes I think tarot card reader can give very specific information as you can ask exact question to tarot card reader and they give answer and sure astrologer can give full prediction of life.'

'Oh I just have no idea.'

'Anyway if you want to meet psychic reader, one tarot card reader whom I consult does this work too.'

'Really?'

'Yes actually one of my classmate wants to talk with her husband, he has died from Corona.'

'Oh sad.'

'Though I don't know online talking is possible or not.'

'Oh.'

'But if you want I can contact to know.'

'Okay if I shall decide, I shall tell you.'

'Okay.'

'Sometimes I think who knows one day if any machine will be invented through which we will be able to connect with dead loved one.'

'Already there are machines like this. I saw on net.'

'But that is different kind of machine…, I imagine if any machine will be invented from which we can see dead person and talk to them…'

Manjulika looked at Soma with a puzzled face and little smile on her face. Soma looked at her, smiled little and said, 'You are thinking I have become mental patient.'

Manjulika's expression became embarrassed then she said, 'No no not at all, no one can tell the future. May be any machine like that will be invented.'

'Actually if any other person said it in front of me then I thought if he or she is mad, but after my mother's death many thoughts come in my mind which I never thought would come in my mind ever.'

'Do you have any fantasy related to Kakima?'

Soma looked at Manjulika with a surprised face then asked in a surprised voice, 'How do you know?'

Manjulika smiled little and said, 'Actually my friend also has a fantasy that her husband has not died, he has gone somewhere keeping a look alike person at his place who died that day, to see how my friend manages everything without him and one day he will come back.'

Soma gave a surprised expression and said, 'Really? You know I also have same kind of fantasy. My mother has gone somewhere keeping a dummy of her to see how I live without her, to make me confident.'

'Oh almost same kind of fantasy.'

'Yes.'

'I think when someone lost any loved person they react in same way. May be people in same situation develop same kind of fantasy.'

'Right.' After a pause Soma said again, 'Anyway I want to talk with tarot card reader once to know if your parents will agree or not for our relation and to know when Corona will be stopped.'

Manjulika smiled little and said, 'Don't know they predict about Corona or not but about relation sure you can ask.'

Soma smiled. After some more talking Manjulika went to her bedroom and chatted some time on Facebook with her two Facebook friends, Sunil and Marius then talked for a long time with Alberto and then after sleeping some time watched a film on net and in evening Rita said she had discussed about Madhulika and Soma's relation with her husband Animesh and they both agreed for the relation. Manjulika made Chicken Curry to celebrate and wrote a poetry at night.

7

∞

Manjulika was sitting in front of dressing-table keeping two lip-colours in front of her. Soma entered into room. 'Oh Soma Di, come.' Manjulika said.

Soma sat on bed and said, 'I am feeling really relaxed.'

'Because Maa and Baba has agreed for your and Didi's relation?'

'Yes.'

Manjulika took a pause and said, 'You know as it is said every bad thing has a good side just like that I think Corona also has some good effects in our life.'

'Like?'

'Like Corona has given us reality check of many things. In which time we think to reach another planet that time we are not safe in our own planet, we can live life not going for hang-out so often, not giving order for food so often, not wasting so much money.'

'Right…'

'Just like that I think Corona has big effect on my parents' minds also.'

'Means?'

'They have understood there is no surety of life so choosing career for children, getting daughter or son married with chosen one by parents or in different gender those things are silly in this world. Ultimate thing is we should be happy.'

Soma took a pause, smiled little then said, 'May be you are right.'

'Okay now you make me happy. Help me to choose one shade of lip-colour.'

Soma smiled little and said, 'Show me.'

Manjulika showed two colours. Soma said, 'Oh one is different kind of light pink and one is light orange.'

'Yes.'

'I think with today's dress light orange will be suitable.'

'I was thinking same.'

'Sure.'

'You know I don't use any deep shade now, as in time of Corona everyone is sad.'

'Yes that is a right choice.'

Manjulika started to apply lip-colour. Soma said, 'Anyway Manjulika after I became so much happy yesterday I could not sleep properly at night and some other days also it happened with me'

Manjulika stopped using lip-colour and smiled little. Soma said, 'But even in this happiness I am little sad.'

'Why?'

'Madhu's birthday is in next week and in time of Corona I can't go to buy anything for her as gift and I don't think any gift shop is opened.'

'So what? We can buy perfume and chocolate from grocery store. Two gifts are found in grocery store also. I am planning to buy.'

Soma took a pause and smiled little and said, 'You are really intelligent.'

Manjulika smiled and said, 'Thanks.'

'Okay I shall buy perfume.' Soma said.

Manjulika smiled.

Soma said took a pause and said, 'Anyway Manju I wanted to tell you something.'

'What?'

'I really have grown up a new interest.'

'What?'

'Tarot card.'

Manjulika smiled.

'Yes actually at mid-night I saw a video on net and I found really interesting.'

'Then sure you can try.'

'My one friend knew a very good astrologer, I wanted to meet him also but he is no more now.'

'Oh.'

'Yes he is no more, died before many years. One of my another friend was making fun hearing it, he died, why astrologer can't stop their own death.'

Manjulika smiled little and said, 'No logic in it. They are astrologers, they can predict whatever written in our horoscopes, with remedies there is a chance they can change little. May be they can get more success in their astrological career with some remedies but they can't be richest person in whole world, they can take remedies before any disease but can't stop death. They are human being their life also goes according to their horoscope and hand lines. How doctors die? Can't they cure themselves and become immoral? Then this question also can come.'

'You sound more logical.'

Manjulika smiled. Soma said, ‘This Corona was also predicted I saw in a video.’

‘Sure.’

‘Anyway once one of my friend said someone did black magic on her and she cured through doing some rituals by a person from occult field. Now I believe.’

‘Sure those things happen.’

‘She guessed her father’s younger brother’s wife did and it came true in tarot card reading.’

‘Natural, unknown people have nothing to do with us, yes only if they want to test themselves how much they have learnt to do black magic then they can try to do it on us.’

‘Right.’

‘Sure those things happen. I also did not think about occult world a lot before but after I get proof now I believe. Can you tell me what is scientifically possible and what is scientifically not possible?’

Soma smiled little, Manjulika said, ‘Sometimes I think if we have not mobile phone we never believed there can be any machine and with that we can talk with people who is far away from us, without any connection or wire.’

‘True.’

‘And science? I think science is created by God and astrology, palmistry are also created by God. May be those things are different types of science. God has written our fate and has given us little chance to change our fate through remedies and free-will.’

Soma smiled. Manjulika said, ‘I think God is the supreme power. Science can say big-bang theory but can say what was before that? Science can find any answer for time, space and causality?’

‘That’s right.’

'Astrology, re-birth all those are written in our book.'

Soma smiled.

'And astrologer and tarot card reader not only predict or give answers, many of them do teaching also. What they teach in classes? Cheating? Then any reporter can go being student and reveal. I never think to try because I have full faith. Astrology is a subject in our country.'

Soma smiled.

'Okay Soma Didi I have to leave.'

'Yes sure sure.'

'Bye.'

'Bye.'

Manjulika left the room, said bye to her parents and left for office booking a car. After going some time she found some dogs were sitting on road, she opened the packet of biscuit, which had brought. She gave some biscuits throwing at side of road. After lockdown was started she started to do it. The driver of that car said, 'Sister, do you like dogs?'

Manjulika smiled little and said, 'Not that much. I love cats more. I used to give food to neighbourhood cats but after lockdown is started I am giving food to dogs also.'

'Oh I also give food to them. Before lockdown I used to feed my neighbourhood dogs only but now I give food to some other dogs also.'

'Nice brother, so how many dogs do you feed?' Manjulika asked.

'Five, five dogs are in our neighbourhood. Some other neighbours also give them food.'

Manjulika thought a poor driver feeding dogs in Corona but her many rich neighbours don't. Actually class, caste, gender, age nothing matters, only people's personality and psychology matter.

After giving biscuits at two other places Manjulika reached office and met one of her collogue Piya at door, Manjulika tried to smile as Manjulika and Piya always had exchanged smile when they had met each-other but Piya did not smile and gave a disturbed look and left. Manjulika hid her surprised expression and continued walking and found almost all collogues were looking at her with disturbed expressions. Manjulika felt confused. For a second she thought her look was okay or not. She knew in her profession looking proper is an important matter. She thought by-chance if new shade of lipstick was not suitable. She was carrying same shade in her bag. She reached washroom as early as possible and could not find anything to change in her look. She came back in the area where her collogues were sitting, she tried to find Nilima but could not find her. Manjulika went near her table and sat. After some time Nilima entered. Manjulika smiled looking at her, Nilima gave disturbed expression but less than other collogues and smiled little and went to her table. Manjulika stood up and found Gautam entered. Gautam gave an expression looking at Manjulika which she had never seen before on Gautam's face and could not read. Manjulika ignored him and went near Nilima. Nilima looked at Manjulika with a disturbed expression. Manjulika felt surprised, took a pause and struggled to find what to say and finally said, 'Nilima...'

Nilima did not reply and kept the same expression. Manjulika took a pause and asked, 'Anything has happened here?'

Nilima replied after a pause, 'Why?'

Manjulika took a pause again and said, 'Don't know why I find everyone's expression is so disturbed though you have come later than me but your expression is also disturbed I find.'

Nilima kept looking at Manjulika few seconds and said, 'Manjulika I did not expect it from you.'

Manjulika became surprised and said in mind, that means my guess is right, everyone is disturbed about me. Manjulika asked, 'What?'

Nilima kept looking at Manjulika few seconds more and said, 'What? How can you do this?'

Manjulika looked at Nilima with a surprised expression and after a pause she asked, 'What yaar? What have I done?' Manjulika started to remember if she has done anything wrong in past few days after asking it.

Nilima's expression became angry, she kept quiet few seconds and said, 'Manjulika I know Gautam disturbed you a lot. I understood your problem totally.'

Manjulika's face became more surprised, she was trying to think why everyone can be disturbed about any matter which was related to Gautam but could not think anything. Nilima said again, 'But his father died because of Corona…, and even if it was not because of Corona then even how can you gave a sign of laugh and write 'Feeing very glad'

Manjulika looked at Nilima with astonished face.

Nilima kept looking at Manjulika. Manjulika was trying to find answer, Nilima asked, 'How can you do this Manjulika?'

'Glad?'

'Yes glad, how can you right this?'

Manjulika kept looking at Nilima with same expression like before. Nilima also kept looking at Manjulika with disturbed face for some time then said, 'Gautam had disturbed you a lot okay but after his father died how can you write like this…, and you gave sign of laugh also.

Manjulika kept quiet few seconds and asked, 'I wrote very glad to know it and gave sign of laugh?'

Nilima kept quiet. Manjulika took a pause and said again, 'And because of that reason you all are angry on me?'

'Should not we be?'

Manjulika took a pause and started to open her Facebook page as she said, 'But I have written sad news and gave sign of cry.'

Nilima's face became confused from disturbed. Manjulika opened her Facebook and then Gautam's page and got surprised, the post about Gautam's father's death was the last post on Gautam's wall. Manjulika saw the post and became surprised, she kept looking some time and said, 'Gad?'

Nilima said, 'Yes gad, by mistake you wrote gad instead of glad we thought.'

Manjulika looked at Nilima with a surprised face and kept looking few seconds and said, 'No I was going to write sad and I think by mistake I wrote gad.' Nilima's face turned confused, after a pause she asked, 'You were going to write sad?'

'Yes yaar, how can I write glad on someone's death even if the person is my biggest enemy?'

Nilima's kept a confused face for few seconds and said, 'I was also thinking how can you write this.'

'But I also did not check properly. I should have checked, really I wrote gad…, I change it now.'

'But what about your laugh sign?'

Manjulika looked at the screen once again and said, 'Yes really I have given laugh sign. That is also by mistake. I was going to give cry sign.'

Nilima looked at Manjulika with a surprised face for few seconds and said, 'OMG and your two mistakes are so matched that we all misunderstood you.'

'Let me change.' Manjulika said again, 'No I don't edit, I delete and write again.'

'Yes that will be better.'

Manjulika deleted the comment and wrote again, 'Very sad news.' and removed the laugh sign and gave cry sign.

Manjulika looked at Nilima after doing that, Nilima also looked at her. After a pause Nilima said, 'OMG I can't believe because of a silly mistake how big misunderstanding is created.'

'Actually two mistakes.'

'Yes because of two mistakes, it seems one.' Nilima said and smiled.

'But now?'

'Now what?'

'Now how shall I make everyone understand?'

'Don't worry.' Nilima stood up and said, 'Hey listen guys…'

Everyone looked at Nilima and everyone's face became disturbed, only Gautam's face was calm. Manjulika guessed Nilima was standing with Manjulika so everyone's face was disturbed and Gautam was most hurt so his face was not disturbed. Manjulika felt bad for Gautam. Nilima said, 'Here is a big misunderstanding about Manjulika.'

Everyone's face became little puzzled. Nilima said, 'We all have misunderstood her.'

Everyone's face became puzzled. Nilima said, 'Whatever we thought she wrote in Gautam's post that was not right, it was a typing mistake and the sign was also given by mistake.'

Everyone kept puzzled faces. Nilima said, 'Actually Manjulika was going to write sad and by mistake she wrote gad and we thought she wanted to write glad and by mistake she wrote gad.' All collogues looked at each-other and after a pause one collogue named Ramesh asked, 'She wrote it by mistake?'

'Yes.' Nilima replied in little firm tone.

'And what about that sign?' One collogue named Manisha asked.

'That was also by mistake. She wanted to give cry sign and by mistake she gave laugh sign and two mistakes were so matched with each-other that we totally misunderstood her.' Nilima said.

All collogues looked at each-other once again. Manjulika found little smile on Gautam's face. Manisha said, 'Who knows now she is telling it. How these kinds of two mistakes happened in same post and why she did not check?'

'Yes I should have checked specially for this kind of serious post.' Manjulika said and looked at Gautam and said, 'I am sorry.'

'It is okay.' Gautam replied with a smile. Manjulika smiled little.

'It is totally a misunderstanding, we should forget it and she has changed the comment and sign both.' Nilima said.

Manisha smiled tauntingly with expression of disbelief on her face and sat on her chair. One by one all collogues sat on chair including Gautam. Manjulika and Nilima looked at each-other. Nilima kept a hand on Manjulika's shoulder and said, 'Forget it.'

Manjulika took a pause and said, 'I can't forget it. Just because of a silly mistake this kind of bad thing has happened. Who believed me or who not don't know. Don't know whole life what all collogues will think about me.'

'Don't think like this. Just forget it. If someone really knows how you are he or she will sure believe you like me.'

Manjulika kept a pale face and went near her table and sat. After some time she went out for shooting and saw a woman to cry sitting on road side. Manjulika went near her and asked, 'Hello!'

The woman looked at Manjulika with surprised face. 'May I know what happened?' Manjulika asked.

The woman kept looking for some time and said, 'I don't have any work for many days. I used to work in four houses as maid and now they don't allow me to go and I am not getting salary.'

Manjulika's face turned pale. The woman said again, 'I have three children at my home. I am widow. I have no one to help me.'

Manjulika felt helpless. The woman broke into tears and said again, 'Corona just has destroyed my life. All responsibilities of my family is on me and I don't have enough money to buy ration even for today.'

Manjulika controlled her emotions and after the shooting with her gave one hundred rupees to that woman and went to some other persons and did shooting with them and gave all of them one hundred rupees and returned home from work and found Madhulika was making chocolate mousse for everyone. Manjulika understood Madhulika was so happy because their parents had agreed for the relation of Madhulika and Soma. Manjulika washed her hands, changed dress and enjoyed chocolate mousse with her parents, Madhulika and Soma then went to her bedroom. After some time Alberto's call came. Manjulika felt thrilled, from last few days she had been planning to say 'Yes' to Alberto. That day she had taken final decision as returning home by car. Manjulika received, 'Hello!'

'Hello dear, how are you?'

'Fine and you?'

'Was okay but after hearing your voice I am fine.'

Manjulika smiled. Alberto's voice came again, 'How is going everything dear?'

'The situation of whole world is so bad. Not so fine but personally at my home situation is okay.'

'Nice, I am also feeling good that my mother is okay now and after many years my mother and father talk to each-other regularly and everything is fine between them now.'

'Very nice.' Manjulika took a pause and said I think Corona has changed many person's mentalities. Many persons understand we fight for small reasons. Many matters of life which seems very very big actually very small. Just the life is how much precious in itself Corona has made us understand.'

'Right but I feel bad many people are dying in whole world. Many people are suffering.'

'Yes not only dying. Many people are suffering, loosing jobs, some businesses are closed. Many people don't have enough money to run family. Study of students are disturbed, specially student of ten, twelve and final years are suffering.'

'Right, here are also many problems.'

Manjulika kept quiet with a pale face. Alberto's voice came again, 'But what about problem of my life Manjulika? Is your mind changed?'

Manjulika felt thrilled, took a pause and asked, 'What do you mean?'

Reply came after some time, 'Have you thought anything about our relation?'

Manjulika took a pause and replied, 'Alberto we are good friends for a long time, I did not think in different way but now I think if you want we can think about a different relation.'

After few seconds reply came, 'Really? Are you serious dear?'

Manjulika smiled and said, 'Yes.'

After a silence reply came again, 'You don't know you have made me how much happy.'

'Yes I thought a lot and found I would be happy with you in my life.'

'I will try my best to make you happy.'

'I will also try to make you happy always.'

'If you will stay whole life with me I will be happy always.'

Manjulika smiled and said, 'But there is a big thing.'

'Our parents?'

'Yes, you have gucssed right.'

'Hope they will agree. When your parents have accepted a partner of same gender for your sister then hope they will agree for us also.'

'I also think same now…, after they agreed for my sister.'

'And hope I shall manage my parents. I don't think it will be tough to manage them. They are quiet liberal.'

Manjulika smiled. Alberto's voice came, 'I love you dear.'

'Thanks.'

'Will not you tell the same?'

Manjulika kept quiet. Alberto's voice came, 'Okay I shall not force you.'

'Thanks for understanding.'

'I shall always try to understand you. I think understanding is a big thing in relation.'

'I also think it.'

Manjulika and Alberto continued talking for one hour.

8

∞

Manjulika was writing a poetry, named Life.

Just after finishing Manjulika read the poetry once and heard ringtone of her mobile. Manjulika knew it was Sobha's call as the ringtone was selected for her. Manjulika received, 'Hello Sobha!'

After a pause reply came, 'Hello!'

'Say how is everything?'

'How are you?'

'In this situation just okay. Corona is just making me depressed and many people are suffering. Though after a long time I just have written a poetry today.'

'Oh nice. Do you have the copy with you?'

'Yes just have written.'

'Please recite.'

Manjulika took a pause and said, 'Okay.'

Life

Life is tough

Life is rough

But can't forget to live

I can't bluff

After a pause Sobha's reply came, 'Wow, very nice. Just within four lines you have written a big philosophy of life.'

Manjulika smiled. Sobha's voice came after some time, 'But Manjulika it is no more philosophy of my life now.'

Manjulika tried to understand meaning of what Sobha had said. Sobha said, 'I really don't want to live any more. I want to do suicide.'

Manjulika felt confused, took a pause and said, 'What?'

After a silence reply came from other side, 'Yes Manjulika I want to do suicide.'

Manjulika felt a shock and then confused and asked, 'Why are you saying like this?'

After a pause reply came from other side, 'Manjulika…'

'Yes.'

'Are you busy now?'

'No, no not at all. You say what has happened.'

'No if you are busy then I can call later. Actually I just want to share with you a serious matter. But if you are doing writing…'

'My writing is finished now and I write when I feel mood for writing. I am totally free now. You say what you want to say.'

No reply came from other side. Manjulika said, 'Hello!'

'Yes.'

'Tell Sobha, please tell, I am worried.'

'Manjulika…'

'Yes.'

'Monthly income of my house is totally stopped.'

Manjulika did not understand what to reply. Sobha's voice came again, 'My father has no earning now from last one month. Somehow one month we have managed from our savings but now it is really difficult for us to do.'

'Oh…' Whatever Manjulika could say.

'We always faced economical difficulties in life but I never thought one day this situation would come…' Sobha's reply came and Manjulika guessed Sobha broke into tears hearing her sound of cry.

Manjulika did not understand what to say. After some time Sobha's voice came, 'You know Manjulika from seven days we are eating one time in a day.'

Manjulika was shaken. After silence from both sides for some time Sobha's voice came, 'Manjulika I want to tell you something.'

Manjulika guessed Sobha would ask money. Manjulika started to think how much she would be able to help. Sobha's voice came, 'I need some money.'

Manjulika was trying to reply something and Sobha's voice came again, 'Listen, I don't want as help, which I would have to return.'

'Okay.'

'Because I don't know I would be able or not to return it ever.'

'Okay, how much do you want?'

'No no I don't want money like this.'

'Then…' Manjulika said being puzzled.

No reply came from other side. For a second Manjulika thought if it would be a huge amount then Manjulika would have to think. Sobha'a reply came after some time, 'Manjulika can you keep me as a maid at your home?'

Manjulika thought for a second if she was hearing something wrong and almost automatically she asked, 'What?'

'Yes Manjulika, I don't think in this situation I can find any job when people are loosing their jobs. But I really want to run my family so I need money, which is most important thing in this world I have understood.'

'Not that always.'

'You have money so you can't understand.'

Manjulika did not reply. After a silence Sobha's voice came, 'Anyway will you keep me as maid?'

'Sobha…'

'Yes will you? I shall not ask a huge amount as salary. Just little to feed my family.'

'Sobha are you serious?'

'Yes.'

'But…'

'Do you have any better option for me?'

Manjulika tried to reply but could not. Sobha's voice came, 'I know you have maid already and you don't need me but if you keep me for any extra work.'

'Sobha…'

'I can massage your parents' feet…, Madhulika's Di's feet also. I can massage your feet also…'

'Sobha…' Manjulika almost shouted.

'So what? I worked as beautician for three months. That time I did pedicure of many youngers.'

'Sobha…'

'Hey remember once I did your manicure and pedicure also.'

Manjulika took a pause and said, 'What are you talking Sobha…'

After a silence reply came, 'I just want to know can you keep me as maid?'

Manjulika did not understand what to reply. Sobha's voice came, 'I really want money Manjulika. I just and just need money to survive in this world.' Manjulika felt bad. Sobha's voice came, 'Manjulika approximately twenty-five kilograms rice is needed for us in a month. I just and just want to secure that for my family. After that we can eat in dinner also once or twice in week from savings.'

Manjulika took a pause and asked, 'Sobha why suddenly so bad situation has come in your life?'

'What a jobless and savings-less family can do? You know twenty-five kilogram rice is my dream now.' Sobha said again, 'Only rice not even salt. For one week no salt is at our home.'

Manjulika was shaken once again and sound of Sobha's crying came from other side. Then her voice came, 'I saw many bad days in life but I never thought one day salt also would be a luxury for us.'

After a pause Manjulika said, 'Sobha I don't understand what to say…'

'We have money to buy salt of some packets but we are afraid to use that. Within some days some religious stuffs to worship of God will be finished. Don't know what we will do. Thanks to God we have some tree for flowers so no need to buy flowers. We give only sugar to God now that also doing counting. Because other items to give are finished already.'

Manjulika kept quiet. Sobha's voice came again, 'My mother always maintain tradition even in our lower-middle class family. She always used lamp mixing little clarified butter with oil but clarified butter or oil is just out of question now, she has shifted to candles from two months but if that will be finished and matchstick will be finished, don't know what will you do.'

Manjulika kept quiet few seconds and said, 'I think God will see your mind, your belief, your prayer, not what you are offering. No one worship at our home regularly, we just pray.'

No reply came from other side. Manjulika said, 'I understand everyone has own religious belief.'

After some time reply came, 'You know my mother's vermilion is almost finished. My mother is using very little vermilion everyday like some girls of this days who use little vermilion to hide marital status.'

Manjulika kept quiet.

'My mother is afraid, after some days…' After this line from Sobha Manjulika heard sound of crying.

Manjulika kept quiet. After few seconds Sobha's voice came, 'Manjulika will you give me job of maid at your house? You tell yes or no.'

Manjulika took a pause and said, 'See Sobha it is not possible for me to keep you as maid.'

Reply came after few seconds, 'You think money will be wasted? Just few months with little salary.'

'It is not about money Sobha. If you want I can help you little…'

'I don't need help. I want work.'

'But how can I keep you? And it is not that easy how much you are thinking. I have to ask my parents also.'

After three seconds reply came, 'Manjulika if Kaku and Kakima don't agree can you keep me as your personal maid or your and Madhulika Di's maid?'

'You want to create division between me and my parents?' Manjulika said in a little angry tone feeling little disturbed.

'No no not at all. You are misunderstanding me.'

'Try to understand Sobha I can't keep you. My parents will not agree how much I know them and I can't keep you personally.' Manjulika made herself calm and replied.

No reply came from other side. Manjulika said, 'And how will you come in time of Corona? Will you stay at my home?'

'Can't I stay for some months?'

'Of-course but not as maid.'

'Manjulika if you keep me you will do a favour on me, you will not insult me.'

Manjulika took a pause and said, 'Sorry it is not possible.'

'You are doing like this with me…'

'See I can keep you as beautician. If you want you can come to massage me everyday for a month but I can't keep you here as maid.' Manjulika said again, 'Okay I shall speak with my mother once, then if she agrees you come and stay at our home for one month as beautician. If you can't come in this time everyday.'

'Manjulika it will be a big favour on me, but by my choice I shall do other works also.'

Manjulika kept quiet some time and said, 'I think if you will work at other places that will be better. Now you don't understand but if you see future then you can see it after some days if everything will be fine and you will get job, you will always remember you worked as maid at your friend's home and it will create problem in our friendship but if you work at any other house then in future if you will get job you will be able to stop all connection with that house.'

'Manjulika are you serious? At first when the situation of this world will be okay no one can say, and please don't ask me to believe your astrologers.'

'Oh common I have not asked any astrologer about it.'

'Anyway so when I shall get job is a big question and where do I find any work of maid in this situation? When people are leaving their permanent maids.'

Manjulika took a pause and asked, 'Are you sure about working at my home as beautician?'

'More than sure.'

'Okay if my mother agrees then I shall keep you as beautician for one month, now as a friend what will you will do at my home that is your choice. Soma Di also does many works.'

'I am very happy that Kaku and Kakima have agreed for your Didi and Soma Di's relation.'

'Me too, the atmosphere of our house is changed.'

'Nice, one good thing in this situation.'

'You know the relation between Alberto's mother and father are also okay now. I think every bad thing has a good side. Many good things are also happening because of it. I understand how much money I wasted visiting malls, restaurants and multiplex. Sometimes sure we visit to enjoy but I wasted money like crazy because I had a very big list to try many restaurants, buying many designer clothes and watching many kinds of films. In this situation those matters seem very silly. That list could be far shorter.'

'You know in my life once I bought a costly dress. I mean costly for me, not for you. It was of one thousand rupees.'

Manjulika smiled little with a pale face and and thought lowest price of her dress is one thousand rupees and highest price is seven thousand rupees which is one designer dress.

Sobha's voice came again, 'I bought make-up box once and some lipsticks, nail-polishes, two eye-liners and now I feel guilty. Guilty for spending money in food court of malls sometimes. If I did not then we had little more savings today.'

'Oh common we have only one life which we should enjoy. Of-course we should save for future and should not waste too much money but you always spent money thinking a lot. I remember very well you thought five times to spend money anywhere. Now who knew this kind of situation would come, we would be part of history. I never wanted to be a part of history in this way though.'

'Me also not.'

'I don't think anyone.'

'You know Manjulika when my parents reached twenty-five years of married life me and my brother were very excited to celebrate. My parents were very reluctant but many relatives also showed interest even two neighbour families also. Finally my parents agreed. You and Kajal also came. We spent fifty thousand rupees approximately. Now those relatives or neighbours don't care about our situation and me and my brother feel guilty.'

Manjulika remembered the celebration.

'If that money was saved as FD then today we can get little more interest. We had thought we would recover money doing job and then suddenly my mother got a need to do an operation and we had to spend money again.'

'No one can calculate so much in life.'

Now I understand celebration of twenty-five years is not for people like us. We should always think to secure twenty-five kilogram rice for month.'

Manjulika felt shaken. Sobha's voice came, 'Manjulika will you inform me today if your mother agrees?'

'Okay I shall.'

If she will agree, tomorrow somehow I shall reach your home. You shall pay me later monthly but tomorrow please for next three days give me daily payment online in the joint account with my mother.'

Manjulika did not understand what to reply. Sobha said, 'If I shall stay there only three persons' food has to be arranged at my home.'

'How much money you want?'

'Seventy-five rupees per day for a month. If everything will be fine I shall try to leave your house as early as possible.'

Manjulika took her another mobile which she had stopped using from last few months and opened calculator and calculate with guilty mind how much money would be for one month. Manjulika found the amount was okay for her after calculation. Sobha's voice came, 'I know Manjulika you don't need maid and it will be extra expenses but that much money I need for my parents and brother.'

'No no okay. You come from tomorrow, if Maa will agree.'

'Will you ask her now and inform me.'

Manjulika took a pause and said, 'Okay you wait for five minutes. I shall call you back after talking with her.'

'Okay.'

Manjulika cut the call and went to her parents' room and found Rita was reading a book. She told her everything about Sobha. Rita at first disagreed for two-three times then said Manjulika can do what she wants. Manjulika retuned into her room and called Sobha, Sobha received just after one ring, 'Hello!'

'Hello Sobha, Maa was reluctant at first, it is natural but finally she has said I can do what I want.'

'Oh…'

Manjulika said after a pause, 'Okay you can come from tomorrow.'

'Thank you, thank you so much Manjulika.'

'You are always welcome. I just want condition of your life and whole world will be okay soon.'

'Really don't know what is waiting for us. Anyway Manjulika where will I stay?'

'You will stay in my bedroom, where else?'

'If you want I can stay in room of maid.'

'You want a slap from me?'

Sound of laugh came from Sobha's side. Manjulika said, 'Just when I talk to Alberto you will have to leave the room.'

'Oho, sure dear. How is going everything?'

'Going nice yaar. Never thought I would be in a relationship with an Italian. I thought about non-bengali but never from anyone who is not from our country.'

'No one can say who is written for whom, you remember the actress from Smita kapoor's serial, who married twice with foreigners. That means every time she has a foreigner in her destiny.'

'I was also thinking about her but I just hope whole life me and Alberto will stay together.'

'I always wish that.'

'But what about you?'

'Yes Thank God Tanmoy has not lost his job. We are planning to marry just after Corona period will be over and I shall get job and hope it will be over soon.'

'Hey does he know you want to come at my home to do job of a maid…, I mean job of a beautician?' Manjulika asked feeling little guilty for using the word maid by mistake.

'He knows I shall do job of a maid. He understands my situation and he wanted to help me but his condition is also not very good and it will be insulting for my parents if they will come to know. I also don't want. He does not have any problem if I shall work at any other home also.'

‘Nice, very nice understanding is between both of you. I hope it will be always between me and Alberto also.’

‘Yes I also think it is most important.’

‘Hey I just want to know have you spoken with Kajal about work?’

‘No yaar how can I ask her? See after all she is not a female and you know situation of her house, her brother and sister-in-law stay with her.’ Sobha said again, ‘And after all they are very formal people. I think they take interviews of maids before keeping them at home. You are also rich but I feel a middle-class atmosphere at your home. What I can ask you that I can’t ask her.’

Manjulika smiled little and said, ‘We are not rich actually, we are upper-middle class.’

‘Oh really?’

‘Sure.’ Manjulika said and smiled once again and saw Kajal was calling her. Manjulika said, ‘Hey what a telepathy, Kajal is calling.’

‘Oh, let’s make conference call.’

‘Yeah.’

Manjulika took Kajal on conference call. ‘Hello!’ Kajal’s voice came.

‘Hello Kajal me and Sobha were talking. I take you on conference call. Sobha is also online.’ Manjulika said.

‘Nice.’ Kajal’s reply came.

‘Sobha’s voice came, ‘Hello Kajal!’

‘Hello!’ Kajal’s voice came.

‘How are you?’ Sobha asked.

After a silence reply came, ‘I am okay, how are you both?’

No reply came from Sobha. 'I am okay.' Manjulika said after few seconds.

Kajal's voice came, 'Today I saw one third of next neighbouhood to be harassed on almost empty road. I know her, I wen t to buy grocery products as almost all servants are on leave. I think I also could face it but I am saved because I look like a female.'

'Don't know why people do this.' Manjulika said.

They three talked some time and Sobha shared her economical condition and she would work at Manjulika's house. Kajal appreciated both of their decision. After talking with both of them for some time Manjulika did lunch and went to terrace and started to walk and found the sky was little more bluish, Manjulika started to walk again after few seconds, after some time Soma came on terrace with some wet clothes. Soma was making hanged those clothes on rope, suddenly Manjulika noticed one maxi and felt little scared. She stopped for three seconds and came near Soma and said, 'Soma Di!'

Soma moved back to Manjulika with a little surprised face and said, 'What?'

'I saw your this maxi with purple colour and same print, but it is yellow. How?'

'I have two same maxis of different colours. But why are you so scared?'

Manjulika smiled little and said, 'Actually I have found the sky is little more bluish today. I have ignored the fact but after I have seen this maxi and I thought if I am shifted to parallel universe.'

Soma giggled and said, 'Oh common, you are really imaginative and always live in fantasy world.'

'Actually right.' Manjulika said and smiled.

'You are writer so you think like this but too much fantasy is also not good.' Soma said as Manjulika started to give watering wo plants which she had planted before some days thinking about global warming and saw a girl of next lane named Manisha to come out on terrace of her house dressing up like a doll. She said, 'But not only writers some other people also live in fantasy world and may be more than me.'

Soma looked at Manisha once and said, 'You are talking about Manisha right?'

'Now she likes to be called Moon only.' Manjulika said and stopped giving water. Soma came near her and both started walking.

'Whatever I think she is a mad actually, otherwise who stay like this, dressing up like a doll always. It is not an ordinary psychological problem, she is becoming mad.' Soma said.

'Don't say like this, please.'

'Becoming mad is not a problem. She can get treatment.'

'But if she is mad then I am also mad.'

'You also want to live like this?'

Manjulika smiled little and said actually when I first saw her change I found very interesting. I thought if I can live like this. Being in this world but not from this world and from different world. Then I realized it is like running from reality, running from problems of this life but that is not so easy. We can't run from reality like this. We have to face challenges and problems of life. We have to take bath, we have to eat, we have to attend nature's call, we have to go to doctor when we become ill. Just wearing a dress, we can't escape from reality how long we live in this world with human body.'

'Right, sometimes I think about her future. Will she get any partner, boy or girl or third gender does not matter, but will she get? Anyone will like any unrealistic girl like her?'

'Who knows, may she is already engaged with any unrealistic person already.'

'May be.' Soma said in a casual tone.

'Or may be with very realistic person who wants a person from totally different mind-setting.'

Soma smiled.

'And not necessary she has to stay with a partner whole life and whatever she sings very well. I must admit.' Manjulika said.

'Yes I also saw three episodes of the reality show where she took came third.'

'I watched all episodes.' Manjulika said and saw Manisha to go inside. Soma said, 'She has gone inside.' Soma suddenly said after few seconds, 'You know actually one day I was thinking what is her opinion about Corona, because she is really unrealistic.'

'May be she thinks if she can stay in different planet this time.'

'Right.'

'Actually in this world many kinds of different people. Some think they are living dolls. In foreign country there are many dolls like this I think. I saw one on you tube. She is singer too and joined a reality show. She also sings very well.'

'Oh really?'

'Yes.'

'Anyway I was watching one episode of Amit Sab Thik Kar Dega.'

'Oh nice serial.'

'There was a girl shown who used to think she is rebirth of a snake and her boyfriend was her partner in past life and he is also rebirth of a snake.'

'Yes yes I remember very well that episode. Who knows really this kind of people are in this world or not.'

'Really.'

'I heard in foreign countries some people marry with car.'

'I also heard.'

'Sometimes I think why we find this kind of people now? Were not they before? In past can we find any story like this?'

'In past rare case we find where people choose partner from same gender. Like me and your Didi.'

'Right.' Manjulika said again, 'I think every kind of people were in every time but because of society they could not say in past I think. At first people became forwarded in western countries then here.'

'Right.'

Anyway are you seeing your favourite serial, 'Global friends and Har Ghar Ek Hi Kahani?'

Soma kept quiet few seconds and said, 'Yes.'

Manjulika and Soma walked and talked some time more and suddenly Soma said, 'Manjulika!'

'Yes.'

Soma took a pause and said, 'You know I am suffering from depression.'

Manjulika looked at Soma with a surprised face and her face became normal and she said, 'Oh from when?'

'Are you not surprised?'

Manjulika smiled and said, 'Why? Just we were talking about many kinds of mentalities. Just like that depression is also part of our mentality.'

Soma smiled little and said, 'I am happy that your parents agreed for our relation but actually staying at home I am feeling depressed. Sometimes I wish if I could go out like you and Madhulika.'

'And I wish if I could stay at home.'

Soma smiled.

'Did you feel depressed before?' Manjulika asked.

'Yes once. That time I did not understand what was happening with me. Then I guessed it is depression and searched on net and symptoms were same.'

'I also faced depression once when I got problem to find suitable jobs.'

'And I felt when my mother became ill first time.'

'Oh.'

'Yesterday one of collogue said his mother has been detected with cancer, in time of Corona he will get many problems to get his mother treated properly.'

'Yes Corona is a new problem in life but all old problems of world are also existing sometimes we forget.'

'Right.'

Manjulika and Soma kept walking some time keeping quiet then suddenly said, 'Hey Soma Di let's cook something together today. You, me and Didi. I think it will help you to recover depression.'

'Okay.'

'Yes not only ordering food or going for hang-out, sometimes cooking at home or doing something what we like we can enjoy and be happy.'

'Sure, nice idea.'

'Actually every bad thing has a good side, Corona has taught us, home is how much enjoyable place for us.'

'That is true.'

Manjulika smiled.

'Anyway what should we cook?' Soma asked.

Manjulika thought little and said, 'Let's make something from western countries.'

'Yes.'

'Let's make Cannelloni.'

'Cannelloni? What is that?'

'Don't you know? One kind of pasta dish. I bought Cannelloni before some days. I was planning to make. Cannelloni is in kitchen and I have everything to make. Milk, cheese, pasta seasoning, mutton and other things. Though I shall not follow the recipe totally, will make in my own way following little.'

'You always do that for savory items.'

'Yes.' Manjulika said and smiled.

'Anyway I ate many western dishes but not Cannelloni.'

'I also never ate in restaurant. I ate once making at home. Let's go to kitchen. We will make together today.'

'Okay.'

'Now you want to go or you want to walk some time more.'

'No no let's go.'

'Okay.'

Manjulika and Soma went to first floor and called Madhulika. Madhulika came out from her room. 'Didi let's cook together today and we will eat in supper.' Manjulika said.

Madhulika looked at Manjulika, smiled little and said, 'Cooking?'

'Yes, today we three will cook together. We don't do much fun activities now. Not going out anywhere for eating-out, to watch film or window shopping. But we will enjoy more at home.' Manjulika said.

‘Sure if we want we can enjoy more at home.’ Madhulika said.

‘We were discussing same and Soma Di is feeling depressed.’ Manjulika said.

‘Yes I know.’ Madhulika said and looked at Soma and smiled.

‘Okay let’s go.’ Manjulika said.

‘Now? No no it will be early. We should make before evening.’ Madhulika said.

‘Yes okay at 5pm?’ Manjulika asked looking at Soma.

‘Yes okay.’ Soma said.

‘Okay then I am going in my room.’ Manjulika said.

‘Okay.’ Soma said.

At 5.05pm Manjulika, Madhulika and Soma went to kitchen. ‘So how Cannelloni is made? I don’t have any idea.’ Madhulika said. Before coming to kitchen Manjulika had said she had plan to make Cannelloni to Madhulika.

Soma said, ‘I also have no idea.’

Manjulika smiled and said, ‘I shall guide you.’

‘You have to.’ Madhulika said and smiled.

Manjulika smiled and took out packet of Cannelloni and said, ‘I have decided to make the whole process in microwave and OTG. No use of gas.’

‘Yes for this kind of items microwave is more appropriate.’ Soma said.

‘Right.’ Madhulika said.

‘Okay we will make one cheese sauce and one tomato sauce and then in tomato sauce I shall put mutton to cook.’ Manjulika said again, ‘Oh and before that will separate little tomato sauce, it will be needed for layering.’

'Okay.' Soma said.

'We have to make white sauce at first to make cheese sauce.' Manjulika said.

'White sauce? I heard of it. How to make it?' Soma asked.

'It will be made with butter, flour, milk, salt and white pepper powder is optional, today I am not going to use that.' Manjulika replied.

'Okay.' Soma said.

'Western sauces are different. From Manjulika I also started to learn something.' Madhulika said.

Soma said, 'I also learned to make some foreign dishes mainly after coming here, hope will learn more if Manjulika will teach me.'

'Sure.' Manjulika said as opened the bottle of cheese powder.

'What is it?' Soma asked.

'Cheddar Cheese powder.' Manjulika said.

'Cheese powder?' Soma asked.

'Yes, I also did not know cheese also has powder version. After Manju bought I have come to know.' Madhulika said.

'Really, I am surprised.' Soma replied and said again after a pause, 'Though why not? When onion, garlic, ginger powders are found then why not cheese? I did not hear about those powders also, have come to know coming here.'

'Really who knew one day we would use onion, garlic powder.' Madhulika said again, 'Though Manjulika just bought for experience otherwise we don't use regularly.'

'Really I am learning about many new ingredients from Manju and western dishes also.' Soma said. Manjulika smiled as washed mutton.

'I know to cook mainly one country's foreign item, Malaysia, because those are have huge similarities between Indian and Malaysian items.' Soma said and smiled. Manjulika and Madhulika joined. Then Manjulika gave direction to make white sauce to Soma and said, 'Though there are many hidden similarities in whole world which we don't know. Marius Uncle showed one item made of coconut which was similar to Narkel Nadu, can you believe?'

'Really surprising?' Madhulika said and she was chopping onion being asked by Manjulika.

'Really.' Soma said

'Tortilla is like our roti.' Manjulika said.

'Hey Manju what is tortilla? I am confused. I also knew tortilla is something like our ruti, Mexican item but that day I saw one person posted a dish of egg and called that tortilla.'

'Yes in Spain or may in Europe one baked dish of egg, almost like baked omelette is called tortilla. First time I also became surprised when I came to know.' Manjulika replied.

'Oh I see.' Soma said.

Manjulika started to chop tomato and said, 'One of my police friend from Brazil was telling children in their country are most afraid of police like here and they behave most politely with them. Human psychology is same everywhere.'

'But that I was reading on net because of curiosity, wearing gold ornaments a lot is not a culture everywhere in world. I don't have to plan to but lot of ornaments in if ever me and Madhu will throw any party to start our relation officially.' Soma said.

'True.' Madhulika said. They three continued talking and Soma said as Manjulika finished spreading grated cheese on the top of uncooked dish, 'Today I am very happy. I have learnt a recipe of foreign country. I like to learn all good things from everywhere.'

'Right I like the globalization concept a lot' Manjulika said. Madhulika and Soma smiled. Manjulika said after few seconds, 'Sometimes I think who knows going to other planets will be easy like visiting other countries and world will play cricket and football and other games with other planets, and name of world's team will be 'WWW' means 'World Will Win.'

Soma smiled and said, 'And we will chant sitting in galaxy of sky, World Will Win, We Will Win.'

Manjulika smiled and said, 'Oh very nice, sure.' Manjulika and Soma high-fived.

'You both are too much.' Madhulika said.

Manjulika and Soma smiled looking at each-other. Then they three hugged together as Manjulika put the dish to cook in OTG.

9

∞

It was one month after Manjulika had stopped using mask. Alberto's parents were totally fine and his father had come to visit his mother and bonding between Manjulika and Alberto had become stronger than before. Sobha's father had gotten his job back. Sobha had said she would go back to her home leaving work of Manjulika's home and would try for new job. Manjulika was happy for her. Kajal had seen some loss in business then his father started to run like before once again. When Sobha had worked at Manjulika's home had given Manjulika head, hand and back massage almost everyday and feet massage three days forcing a lot. She had been taking care of Manjulika's dresses and imitation ornaments, watches and cosmetics, in which work Manjulika was not expert. One day Manjulika had shouted on Sobha for being late to clean her bed. Sobha had not reacted and had come quickly to clean and Manjulika had felt very bad had asked forgiveness. Sobha had smiled and had said, 'It is totally fine.' It was the day Sobha would leave Manjulika's house. Sobha was sitting on Manjulika's bed in Manjulika's bedroom, said, 'Manjulika…'

'Yes.' Manjulika replied.

Sobha took a pause of few seconds and wiped her tears and said, 'Thank you so much Manjulika for helping me in this situation.'

Manjulika could not understand what to reply, she smiled very little, forcefully. Sobha said, 'You have proved you are a true friend.'

Manjulika found a reply, she said, 'Sobha real friends come to help in bad situations, Kajal also tried from her side. She also wanted to help you money.'

'Right, but everyone can't be this kind of true friend.'

Manjulika smiled little and after a pause said, 'You know I also enjoyed a lot when you stayed here. When I was on the way to return home from work I always thought now I have a friend at home, just after going I would talk with a friend, would share everything of whole day, different experiences of Corona time.'

Sobha smiled little and said, 'I feel overwhelmed if I could give you little happiness.'

Manjulika gave an embarrassed smile. Sobha said, 'You know I have two rich friends from neighbourhood and many rich relatives but I knew no one would help me other than you and Kajal but I could not ask Kajal.'

Manjulika smiled. Sobha met with Manjulika's parents, Madhulika, Soma and left. Manjulika returned from main gate and called Alberto. After two rings Manjulika heard Alberto's voice, 'Hello darling!'

'Hello dear!'

'What a co-incidence I was just going to call you.'

'Oh.'

'I want to tell you something.'

'Sure.'

'You know my parents are going to get married again.'

Manjulika took a pause and said, 'What?'

After a pause reply came, 'Yes, yesterday my father came at our home with one bunch roses.'

'Wow!'

'And then my parents went for dinner.'

'Wow!'

'Actually dinner was my idea. I think I am becoming romantic day by day.' Manjulika smiled. Alberto said, 'I think it is effect of you.' Manjulika smiled more. Alberto said, 'I booked a table for them in that restaurant where they went for first date.'

'Wow!'

'After they returned I find they were very happy. My father stayed with me at night in my room.'

'Oh, he is at your home now?'

'Yes he will return today in evening and after registry he will stay here some time and we will stay sometimes at his house also.'

'Very nice.'

After a pause reply came, 'And I have one other good news.'

'What?' Manjulika said as she thought if good news was Alberto had made his parents agree for Manjulika and Alberto's relation. Alberto said, 'This morning I talked to my parents about you.' Manjulika smiled. Alberto said again, 'I thought I would have to talk with both of them differently and I never thought I would able to talk with both of them together. I am feeling so happy dear.'

Manjulika smiled and waited for Alberto to tell what his parents had replied. Alberto said, 'I showed your photo to both of them and said about our relation.'

Manjulika wanted to ask what they had said but controlled herself. Alberto's voice came, 'At first they were surprised but within five minutes they agreed and seeing your photo, they said she is pure Indian beauty.'

Manjulika felt thrilled.

Alberto's voice came again, 'They asked if we are from same belief and they are happy hearing we are from same belief. Though for me only you are important.'

Manjulika smiled and said, 'I think my parents we will be surprised and happy hearing we are from same belief.'

'Good.' Alberto said again, 'Anyway they have said they want to meet you soon.'

Manjulika took a pause and said, 'I am also planning to tell my parents soon.'

'Very good.'

'As I said we are planning to visit some countries of Europe. Today I talked with Didi and Soma Di and I shall talk with my parents soon. Hope we will meet soon.'

'Sure dear.'

'Actually my parents had agreed for relation between my Didi and Soma Di and we are planning to make small party with close friends and relatives to start their relation formally as situation is becoming normal after Corona.'

'Oh nice.'

'After that I am planning to tell.'

'Hope they will also agree easily.'

'Hope so.'

'I shall pray a lot. After my parents have planned to marry again I have developed a big faith in God. Now I regular pray.'

'Very good yaar.'

'And you have come in my life that is also a big reason.'

Manjulika smiled. Alberto said, 'If you will come in my life forever, my will be completed.'

Manjulika smiled and said, 'But Alberto I think we should meet once at first.' Manjulika took a pause and said again, 'I shall have to tell my parents before going to Italy because I can't give them a shock going there but I think we should take final decision meeting face to face once.'

'I also have told my parents I shall take final decision after meeting her once and I also wanted to inform at first.'

'Yes one of the biggest decision of life we can't take not meeting with each-other.'

'Actually I think I already have taken decision, just formally we should meet.'

Manjulika smiled little and asked, 'Anyway how is health condition of your parents?'

'They both are fine now and your parents?'

'They are also fine.'

'Anyway Manju, if you don't mind may I ask you a question?'

'Sure.' Manjulika said with a confused mind.

'I heard your family is little conservative so where Madhulika Didi and Soma Di stay? In same room?'

Manjulika smiled little and felt good hearing Alberto to call Madhulika as Didi and Soma as Di. In next second Manjulika felt thrilled thinking Alberto started to think so deeply. Manjulika took a pause and said, 'Before my parents had come to know about their relation Soma Di was staying with my Didi in same room and after my parents came to know they never asked to stay Soma Di in different room.' Manjulika took a pause and said again, 'After all they are belonging from same gender so may be the matter is little easy.'

'Okay understand.' After few seconds Alberto asked, 'Hey Manjulika do you have any lesbian friend?'

'Yes three on Facebook.'

'Oh I also have one gay friend though from different country, on Facebook. But we are just friend.' Manjulika heard Alberto's voice and laugh with that. Manjulika joined laughing and said, 'Sure, actually I find there is nothing wrong to make friendship with any lesbian for a girl or to make friendship with any gay for a boy.'

'Sure.'

'If a girl is straight that does not mean she feels special feeling about every boy just like that if a girl is lesbian does not mean she is attracted to every girl. For me Soma is just like an elder sister.'

'Sure and same goes for gay boys.'

'Yes.'

'Hey dear if you don't mind can we talk later? One of my friend is calling. I know he has some urgent need about business.'

'Sure dear. We will talk later.'

'Okay in evening, within 7pm to 7,30pm of your country I shall call, okay?'

'Sure.'

'Okay bye dear.'

'Bye.' Manjulika cut the call and opened laptop and started to play chess. In first round she lost. In next game she won with different player with just two moves playing with white pieces. Opponent's message came, 'Hi dear!'

'Hi!'

'What was it?'

'Two moves, in one situation just with two moves with white pieces we can win.'

'Omg I never had any idea.'

'Okay want to play once more?'

'I am scared but sure.'

'Okay.'

Manjulika started to play once more and won after twenty moves. Message came from opponent, 'Played nice.'

'Thank you bye.'

'Bye.'

Manjulika left and switched off laptop. After watching Tarun Mehra Ka Ulta Chasma for some time Manjulika took bath and ate and left for office. She had a little late schedule for that day. After reaching the first signal by bus Manjulika found her five years' senior student from her school Ruma's call came. Manjulika received after three rings, 'Hello!'

'Hello Manjulika this is Ruma.'

'Yes your number is saved, say.'

'Are you free now?'

'Yes I am going to office. I am in bus, you say.'

'Oh Okay.' Manjulika heard the reply then no other word came from other side. Manjulika said, 'Hello!'

'Yes hello!'

'What happened?'

'Manjulika how is everything?'

'After Corona period feeling little better.'

'Some people's pain never ends even after Corona.'

Manjulika tried to understand what Ruma had tried to say. Ruma's voice came again, 'Manjulika can you do a favour on me.'

'Favour?' Manjulika asked being little worried thinking if Ruma would ask money.

'Yes can you give me little money?' Ruma's voice came.

'Money? Little? How much?'

'Manjulika I know you kept Sobha as maid.' Manjulika felt a shock. She and Sobha and Kajal had decided to keep the matter secret from any other persons of school and she had not shared with anyone. For a second Kajal's name came in her mind for disclosing. Manjulika asked, 'How do you know?'

'Your one maid Kobita who comes at your home everyday and my brother-in-law's maid are friends. My sister-in-law told me.'

'Oh.' Manjulika replied and felt guilty for thinking Kajal's name for disclosing. Manjulika said, 'Anyway so what?'

After few seconds reply came, 'Manjulika can you give five hundred rupees? I shall return.'

'Five hundred?' Manjulika said as thought anyone can ask only five hundred? Which amount was not at all a big amount for her. She had thought Ruma would ask at-least five thousand and Manjulika would agree for two thousand only. Ruma's reply came, 'Yes five hundred. I know it is a big amount but if you help me.'

'Five hundred? Okay I can manage but may I know why?'

After few seconds reply came, 'Actually I have lost my job.'

'Oh.'

'I am managing somehow and trying for new job but in this time I really need five hundred suddenly extra.'

'Okay.'

After few seconds reply came again, 'Actually I want to give my daughter a doll.'

'Doll?'

'Yes, actually you know my condition very well. After my husband's death I was alone managing the family with job of a small amount salary. I was planning to give her a doll last birthday which she had liked very much.'

'Okay.'

'Because I could not give her even one doll when she was child.'

Manjulika did not understand what to reply. Ruma's voice came, 'She is twelve now. Already age to play with dolls is passed and I forcefully kept her childhood and she too.'

Manjulika felt goosebumps. Ruma said again, 'I was planning to give her in twelfth birthday but could not and next week she will be thirteen. Teenage, and If I can't give now it will be too late. So…'

'I will sure give. Can you take online payment?'

'Why not? Actually Doll does not cost five hundred, I want to buy one cake and will make Payesh and some other items which she likes, very rare I can make any item which she likes. I have little money and I want five hundred more.'

'Okay I will pay you today and when is her exact birthday?'

'Next Monday.'

'Okay wish her happy birthday from my side in advance.'

'Thanks but when I shall be able to return I don't know.'

'Don't worry at all.'

'Okay and everything fine?'

'Yes almost fine.'

'I am very happy your parents have agreed for your Didi and her partner's relation.'

Manjulika felt a shock once again and asked almost instinctively, 'How you…'

'Same, maids' discussion. Your maid Mithu who stays whole day said to Kobita.'

Manjulika first time realized her family's maids Mithu and Kobita understand the relation between Madhulika and Soma. Before that she had thought they do not understand anything. Manjulika felt little angry on Mithu and Kobita and replied to Ruma, 'Yes I am also happy my parents have agreed for them.'

'I totally understand some people have feeling about same gender.'

'Yes good you understand.'

'But what about you? When you are becoming engaged?'

'Let's see.' Manjulika said and smiled.

'Okay, okay.'

'Okay I shall pay in evening. Should I pay in this number?'

'Yes.'

'Okay will talk later. Bye.'

'Bye.'

Manjulika cut the call and suddenly got tears in her eyes, she wiped tears and decided she would try to fulfill one dream of one person in every year. After some time she reached office and met Gautam just after entered, Gautam had never disturbed her again after the misunderstanding between Manjulika and Gautam had been cleared. They just have talked sometimes. Gautam smiled looking at her, she smiled back and reached near her table and sat. Nilima came near her, Manjulika talked with her some time and left for shooting with photographer Turna. Going after some time Manjulika bought one packet of chips. Manjulika and Turna both sanitized their hands and started to eat chips. Turna said, 'How our life and mentality are changed after Corona. Now we don't eat anything not using sanitizer.'

'Yes not about this matter, about many matters.'

'You know one of my cousin used to disturb girl a lot.'

Manjulika looked at Turna with surprised face. Turna looked at her and said, 'Yes I never liked him but after Corona he has stopped that and trying for job to take responsibility of family.'

'Oh nice.'

'I saw him to disturb neighbourhood girls who wear kurta, leggings but not any girl who wears jeans, t-shirt.'

'Same experience I have as I told you. In college everyday I went wearing salwar-kamiz and was disturbed a lot but never in shopping mall wearing jeans-t-shirt.'

'You know sometimes boys are also harassed by boys or girls in workplaces and at some other places.'

'True.'

After some time Manjulika reached shooting places and started to take opinion of some people for the serial Tarun Mehra Ka Ulta Chasma where the character Chiriyalal who had been unmarried for a long time finally had gotten married with a foreigner Olivia. Manjulika asked a girl named Riya Ghosh and got her opinion, 'I am very happy seeing Chiriyalal is married finally and with a foreigner but from same belief.' Manjulika smiled little thinking about her and Alberto's relation. Riya said again, 'Now one woman who is from our country but looking a foreigner and one is real foreigner will stay in same building. I am super-duper excited to see upcoming episodes.' Manjulika smiled more then finishing shooting reached home in evening and found Madhulika had reached before her. Soma entered in her room after some time and said, 'Manju me and Madhu have done some planning for party for starting our relation officially but need to discuss with you.' Manjulika smiled.

'Not asking you we will not do anything. You are great planner for party.' Soma said.

'Sure I also have made some plans. I was also waiting.' Manjulika said. Madhulika entered in Manjulika's room and they three discussed about plans and then Manjulika started to invite and she called Rahul's Punjabi wife Natasha whom he had gotten married before one month. Natasha's voice came after three rings, 'Hello Manju, how are you dear?'

'Fine, you say how are you? How is going your new married life?'

'Yes fine.'

'Good, I have called you to invite for a party.'

'Party.'

'Yes Didi and Soma Di are starting their relation officially and before that they want to throw a party.'

Oh I am very excited. Once I attend where a couple gave party to start live together and here both are from same gender. I am really very excited.'

Manjulika smiled and said, 'Inform Rahul and my mother will call Rahul's mother Kakima to invite your in-laws but still I call to invite both of you.'

'Nice.'

'You say where are going for honeymoon?'

'We are planning Switzerland.'

'Oh nice.'

'But my mother-in-law is telling huge amount will be wasted. But if me and Rahul will pay what is her problem? Mother-in-laws are same everywhere, community does not matter.'

Manjulika thought for a second how would be Alberto's mother and asked, 'Are you getting problem with Kakima?'

'Sure, she always gives hint I have gotten my husband for her, why does she forget Rahul has gotten wife for my parents. Boys also need life partner, any boy does not marry any girl to give the girl a security for whole life.'

'Sure.'

'Rahul's mother says whole life I worked at home. Why does she forget whole life she spent husband's money and kept maid.'

'Sure, work done by maid is done by the working boy or working girl of the house indirectly because salary is paid from their salary.'

'Yes if they are home-maker are we home-breaker? We all are home-makers, they are full-time and we are part-time.'

'Totally agree.' Manjulika talked with Natahsa some more then cut and played online Ludo for some time then watched some videos on laptop and found Alberto had called her five times on another mobile which was on silent mode. Manjulika felt surprised as she could not remember when she had done it. Manjulika called him back. After seven rings Alberto's voice came, 'Hello!'

'Hello!'

'Say!'

Manjulika took a pause and guessed Alberto was angry. She and Alberto had quarreled with each-other two times. Manjulika knew how Alberto reacted when he was angry. Manjulika took a pause and said, 'You called five times I just have seen.' No reply came from other side. Manjulika took a pause and said, 'I am sorry dear. Actually I was playing Ludo and then watched some videos on net.'

'So what? Just you could not receive my call?'

'Don't know how my mobile went on silent mode.'

'Oh.'

'I am sorry.'

'But you knew I can call. We decided to talk this time.'

'Dear but I really forgot.'

'Forgot? And you are telling that proudly?'

'Alberto why are you talking like this?'

'Because I felt so.'

'Alberto please…'

'What please? In morning we decided to talk and you just forgot.'

'Oh come on yaar. I am sorry.'

'When you say like this I feel you are neglecting me. I feel very bad.'

'You are doing too much. I think you are becoming more emotional than me sometimes.'

'Manju we will talk later.'

'Alberto…' Manjulika said and understood Alberto had cut the call. Manjulika felt little guilty, little sad, little angry. She opened Facebook and found a post, 'Where asking dowry is wrong their asking govt. job holder groom right, how?'

'Boys also can ask govt. job holder bride, as they ask, full-time home-maker, job holder, job-holder more preferable, docile, expert in house-hold works, educated, good-looking, fair, job-holder and homely bride but till now I did not see any girls' parents to ask an amount from bank balance of groom's parents which boys family ask as dowry.' After doing the post Manjulika felt relaxed and saw message from her Laali from Uganda, 'Hi dear!'

'Hi how r u!' Manjulika replied.

'Fine dear and u?'

'Fine and how is everyone at ur home?'

'All are fine and at ur home?'

'Fine.'

'Ok.'

'So are you planning to go to do job in foreign country?'

'Yes.'

'Very good, all the best. Good that you have overcome after loosing money.' Laali had said Manjulika she loses a huge amount of savings before some days.

'Sure, we have hands and legs, we will earn once again.'

'Very good.'

'How is ur relation going with Alberto?'

Manjulika remembered the quarrel between her and Alberto. She thought it was a casual matter, she smiled little and wrote, 'Very fine.'

Manjulika chat with Laali some time and then saw one video on Facebook and tried to sleep but could not sleep. She felt an urge to talk with Alberto again and again. She made some imagination with him about tour in some places of Kolkata and Rome. She felt little good and once again she felt bad and did masturbation with her most favourite fantasy of that time, becoming dominated by a dominating girl from her classmates of school with whom she rare spoke on Facebook after leaving school and had rare spoken in school. Once in school she had been dominated by her going to do verbal fight and had not enjoyed at all in reality. At 3am she suddenly looked at clock and felt little scared as she had heard 3am was 'Devil's hour.' She closed her eyes and slept at 3.45am and woke up at 5am hearing ringtone of her mobile. She understood it was Alberto's call as the tone was selected for him. She received, 'Hello!'

'Hello dear are you angry on me?'

'No dear not at all. It was my fault. Are you angry on me?'

'No dear actually I could not sleep at all, here is midnight now.'

'Here is morning, 5am. I also could not sleep properly. Just have slept.'

'Oh no, I have made you wake up.'

'No no okay. I am feeling good after talking with you.'

'I am really sorry dear.'

'I am sorry too.'

'Totally fine dear.'

'And in future we will try not to quarrel on small matters like today.'

'Then you want us to quarrel for big matters?'

'Very funny.' Manjulika said in a false angry tone and laughed and heard laugh from Alberto's side. Manjulika said, 'Okay dear we should try to sleep now. We will talk tomorrow evening at same time which we decided for yesterday.

'Totally agree dear.' Alberto's reply came.

'Okay bye dear.' Manjulika said.

'Bye dear.'

Manjulika cut the call and tried to sleep and slept after half an hour then okay up at 9am, after taking bed tea, being ready, taking lunch leave for office and in evening called Alberto on decided time and talked with him for one hour. Just after cutting the call she found her neighbor friend Bristi was calling. A conversation happened between them after Manjulika received, 'Hello!'

'Hello!'

'Yeah Bristi say.'

'How are you?'

'Fine and you?'

'Not at all fine. Many problems in life.'

'Yes I know.' Manjulika knew her friend Bristi had problem about relationship in her life.

'I am feeling depressed.'

'I understand.'

'I have called to meet with Tarot Card Reader. You told me about one Tarot Card Reader.'

'Yes very good, she is doing study in astrology also.'

'Yes yes, I want to take an appointment.'

'I am also planning to meet her. We can go together.'

'Why not?'

'I shall talk with her. Anyway when you are free?'

'Sunday will be good.'

'For me too. Okay I shall talk with her about date and after talking with you once, I shall finalize.'

'Sure.'

'Okay I shall inform you. Bye.'

'Bye.'

Manjulika cut the call and started to read a novel, 'Love Before & After Corona.'

10

Manjulika was sitting on bed with her mother Rita in bedroom of her parents. Rita was sitting in front of her and father was sitting on a chair beside the bed. Rita had asked her for marriage once, after officially Madhulika and Soma had started to live together giving party. Manjulika had said Rita she would talk with her mother and father Animesh together after few days. That day she wanted to talk. Rita and Animesh were looking at her with serious faces. Manjulika kept quiet some time. Rita asked, 'Is anyone in your life?'

Manjulika looked at Rita, she found Rita's face was very serious, she tried to find shadow of anger but could not. Manjulika kept looking at her few seconds then said, 'Yes Maa and there is nothing wrong today.'

Rita smiled little, Animesh's face became more serious. Rita asked, 'What is his name? How do you know him?'

Manjulika thought the foreign name would give them a shock, she decided to tell something about Alberto at first. She kept quiet few seconds and said, 'He is an Italian.'

Rita and Animesh both looked at her with surprised faces. After few seconds Rita asked, 'Italian?'

Manjulika had expected this expression but felt little uneasy. She took few seconds to gain courage and said, 'Yes Maa he is an Italian but he is from our belief. By chance they are also following same belief even after being foreigner.'

Rita and Animesh's expressions became puzzled, both looked at each-other. Manjulika prepared herself and said, 'His name is Alberto Magnani. He is Italian and doing business of leather.'

Rita and Animesh kept looking at Manjulika for few seconds then Rita looked at Animesh, Animesh looked back at Rita. Both looked some time at each-other then Rita looked Manjulika and asked, 'From our belief? Means Italian lives in Kolkata? His ancestral are from Italy?'

Manjulika took a pause and said, 'No they live in Italy. But his ancestral are also from Italy but his ancestral came back to our religion.' Rita's face turned puzzled. Manjulika said, 'Actually when I talked to Marius Uncle I find their old belief had many similarities with our belief, like burning bodies after death, and wearing white instead of black when someone dies and worshipping idols. Some people say whole world was belonging from our belief in past and Alberto's ancestral had found that similarities so they had taken.'

Rita and Animesh kept looking at Manjulika with puzzled faces some time then Animesh smiled little. Rita kept the puzzled face some more time and asked, 'Whatever that means they are foreigners?'

'Yes, Alberto and his parents live in Italy.'

Rita's face became little scared, she looked at Animesh, Animesh gave a puzzled smile. Rita looked at Manjulika and said, 'And how do you know him?'

'From Facebook and after that we are talking for a long time on phone. He sent me one card also and I told one of my aged friend whom I call Uncle had sent and I showed you a different store-bought card. Sorry for that.' Rita and Animesh's faces became little angry. Then Manjulika said again, 'He has Bengali neighbor from Kolkata there and that neighbour is planning to marry an Italian girl there. Alberto has good friendship with him and Alberto knows and remembers a lot about our culture. Rituals of our beliefs are practiced at his home.'

Rita kept looking at Manjulika few seconds and asked, 'After marriage you will be settled in Italy?'

'Not that, we will stay some time here and some time there. His parents are also willing to visit our country.'

Rita gave a pale look at Manjulika. Manjulika gave worried look at Rita. Rita and Animesh both kept quiet some time then Rita said, 'But he is from Italy, foreigners, so what if he is from our belief, when you went so far? How long you are in relationship?'

'Approximately two years. At first we were friends.'

'And now you are telling me? But you always said you never hide anything from me.'

Manjulika gave a smile and little shame was visible on her face, then she said, 'Maa who tells this from beginning about this kind of matter?'

Rita smiled. 'Didi also did not tell about Soma Di before.' Manjulika said. Rita smiled more. After a silence Animesh said, 'Why do you want to marry an Italian boy?'

Manjulika kept quiet. Rita looked at Animesh once then smiled little looking at Manjulika. Animesh asked, 'And what the boy's parents say?'

'They also felt surprised but then they agreed very easily.' Manjulika replied.

'May be not a big deal for them.' Rita said.

Manjulika kept quiet. Rita said after some time, 'Could not you like any Bengali boy? Or at least from our country?'

'If I liked non-bengali boy then you could say could not you like any bengali boy. Today I am liking a foreigner so you are keeping non-bengali also as an option.'

Rita smiled little with little angry expression. Manjulika said, 'Maa I also never thought but it was destiny.'

Rita and Animesh gave puzzled smile. Manjulika said, 'Life does not go as you thought. Two plus two are not four always. Not necessary I am bengali so I shall have to like one bengali.'

'But culture and mentality matches between same community.' Rita said.

'That's also not necessary, after talking with many foreigners on Facebook and making friendship with them on Facebook I understand human nature are somehow same everywhere.' Manjulika said again, 'Bonding between husband-wife and parents and children are same like us.' Rita and Animesh kept same expression. Manjulika said, 'You know there also younger respect elders but now it is not found so easily and teachers beat student before and now it is stopped and some parents beat till now, legal, illegal does not matter.'

Rita smiled little, Animesh kept a serious face. Suddenly Rita said, 'How does he look like?'

'Let me show his photo. Manjulika said and opened his photo on mobile gave the mobile to Rita. Rita saw some time, smiled little then gave to Animesh and he saw some time and smiled less than Rita and returned the mobile to Rita and Rita to Manjulika. Rita took a pause and said, 'He is good looking and somehow matched with Indian look.' Manjulika smiled and Animesh also. After a silence Rita said, 'But suddenly an Italian boy, you never met with him…'

'Maa we have decided to marry but sure we will take final decision after meeting once. So I want when we will go to visit some countries of Europe for tour then we will meet each-other and you both will meet Alberto's parents.'

Rita and Animesh looked at each-other. Manjulika, Rita and Animesh kept quiet almost half minutes then Rita said, 'Your Didi choose a different kind of life-style and you also have chosen a different kind of life-style. Why this has happened with us?'

Manjulika felt little guilty. Rita and Animesh kept quiet some time then Rita said, 'After meeting with him if you will not find any problem, are you sure to marry him?'

'Yes totally, otherwise why I have gone so far with a foreigner.' Manjulika replied.

Rita took a pause and looked at Animesh. Animesh looked at Rita some time then said, 'I don't understand anything. You say.' Rita's face became worried. Manjulika tried to tell something to make the atmosphere better but could not find anything. After some more silence Rita said, 'That means I shall not get any daughter married with a life partner as I expected.'

Manjulika felt guilty once again then said, 'Maa if I chose anyone like Didi means from our country but from same gender then did you feel better?' After telling it Manjulika felt little guilty because she thought she was blaming her elder sister's choice somehow. Rita looked at Animesh and Animesh looked at Rita. Manjulika said again, 'And if I chose anyone from our country but different belief, I mean people who are from our country but keeping foreign belief, if I chose anyone from them, was it better?'

'But could not you choose any boy from our country and same belief?' Rita asked.

'I also wanted Maa, I always wanted, but it was destiny.' Manjulika replied. Animesh stood up and said, 'You both talk I am going to ground floor now.' Manjulika and Rita looked at Animesh once. Animesh left the room. Manjulika and Rita kept quiet some time then Manjulika went near Rita and hugged her. Rita smiled little. Manjulika said, 'Maa I also feel very bad. Didi has taken so-called different kind of choice from society and I have chosen an Italian boy but Maa we really feel we will stay together happy.'

Rita kept quiet. Manjulika said again, 'As you know many boys proposed me in neighbourhood, in college, university, coaching classes, in office and on Facebook also but when I find he is suitable for me then I agreed.'

Rita kept quiet some time then said, 'But Italian boy…' Rita took a pause and said again, 'And if I should not say anything but after meeting you both will find you both are not suitable for each-other and if you will not be able to stay with him in future then any boy from here will marry you?'

Manjulika felt a shock, she kept looking at Rita few seconds and then thought about the matter and then said, 'Maa you always taught me, in life always two plus two is not four. Didi also believe it.' Rita looked at Manjulika. Manjulika said, 'See Maa after doing arrange marriage just meeting with Baba once at your home and not talking even once you are living a happy life with Baba and your one cousin sister did love marriage being in relationship for five years but divorced within two years.' Rita smiled little. Manjulika took a pause and said again, 'My school friend Sobha always did better result than me in school but today I am doing better job than her.' Manjulika felt little guilty giving that example. Rita smiled little. Manjulika and Rita both kept quiet some time then Rita said, 'But does he want to marry you because you are belonging from same belief? May be finding any girl from same belief in their country is difficult for him.'

'No Maa, I can feel it is not any reason. He also said it.'

'Okay you go now, we will talk later and will talk more in detail.' Manjulika tried to say something but could not find even one word, she smiled little with worried expression for few seconds then left.

11

Manjulika's parents had agreed about Manjulika and Alberto's relation after one day after Manjulika had informed her parents about Alberto. Manjulika, Madhulika, Soma were sitting in a room of Manjulika's Facebook friend Sunil's house. Sunil and his wife Babita were sitting in front of them. Sunil's son Gaurav and daughter Anshu came. Sunil introduced them with Manjulika, Madhulika and Soma. Manjulika asked their school name and class and then they left. Manjulika, Madhulika, their parents and Soma were going to visit four countries of Europe. Before that they were staying in Delhi for one day in a hotel. Manjulika, Madhulika and Soma went to meet Manjulika's Facebook friend Sunil and his family who were staying in Delhi. Manjulika said, 'So finally we meet.'

Sunil and Babita smiled.

Manjulika took out the gift from bag which she had bought for Sunil and his wife then gave the gift it to them. After talking some more Manjulika, Madhulika and Soma did lunch there and left. Reaching hotel, they three took rest for some time lying on bed then Manjulika opened the mobile and saw three friend requests, Manjulika did not find interesting and did not accept and then checked messages and found one from her Australian friend Olivia Culpo, 'Hi how r u?' Manjulika found she was not online. Manjulika replied, 'I am fine. Me and family are going to visit four countries of Europe for tour, how are you?' and checked next message from one of her friend Ricky Umali from Philippines, 'Hi how r u? How is everyone in your family? What about your Europe tour?' Manjulika found he was not online.

'I am fine and everyone is fine in my family. Now we are in Delhi. Tomorrow we will leave for Europe. How is everyone in ur family?' Manjulika checked notifications and kept the mobile on bed-side table and heard Soma to say, 'Madhu I am feeling little worried.' Madhulika was lying beside Manjulika and Soma was lying after Madhulika. Madhulika asked in a curious voice, 'Why?'

After few seconds Soma's reply came, 'I am afraid. I know English but rare spoke in life. So I am afraid.'

'So what? We will be with you.' Madhulika said.

'Actually how much I came to know from my foreigner friends, ten percent of European know English properly and some knows but don't speak. We should use Google translator if possible.' Manjulika said.

'It will be very helpful if it will be possible.' Soma said.

'I spoke in English with Alberto and with Marius Uncle also but very rare, but chatted with many persons.' Manjulika said.

'I spoke sometimes but chatted rare as I don't chat generally on social media with any unknown.' Madhulika said.

'I never chatted with unknown.' Soma said.

'No problem I am with you.' Madhulika said. Manjulika smiled.

'But really how many misconceptions we have about many things. I always thought all European know fluent English. Now I have come to know many Europeans also get problem to speak in English.' Soma said.

'Many misconceptions we have. You know one of my friend from USA said he does not want his daughter to wear very short dresses. I never thought I would hear any American father to speak like Indian father.' Manjulika said.

'Really?' Soma asked.

'Yes my one friend of Facebook said. He is from USA.' Manjulika replied.

'Strange.' Soma said.

'And once said he does not want to visit Las Vegas as it is not a place for a person of his age. He is sixty-one, and he says he does not like junk food.' Manjulika said.

'Really surprising.' Soma said.

'Yes somewhere we all are same. Human mentality is same somewhere. I think so you and Alberto are in relationship.' Madhulika said.

Manjulika smiled.

'Though I never thought you would choose any Italian boy.' Madhulika said.

'I also never had thought you would choose any girl before I come to know about you.' Manjulika said and giggled.

'Shut up.' Madhulika said and smiled, Soma giggled. 'Anyway we have taken everything right? Otherwise we can buy from here.' Madhulika said.

'No no I have taken everything. What about you?' Manjulika said.

'I also have taken. You need anything to buy?' Madhulika asked looking at Soma.

'I also have taken.' Soma said.

'You have taken cream? There cream will be needed sure I think, cold weather.' Manjulika asked looking Madhulika.

'My skin is oily but I also have taken. Don't know Maa has taken or not.' Madhulika said.

'She can use is from us.' Manjulika said.

'Yes.' Madhulika replied.

After a silence Soma said, 'I am very very excited to visit foreign countries. I always thought how is world outside India.'

'Same here.' Manjulika said.

'I am not that excited. I am just happy that after a long time I shall enjoy a tour, will spend some time with my family and will get rest from my work.' Madhulika said.

'Actually I always thought how is outside world, just like us? Are there houses, hotels, malls just like us, standing on ground or anything else? Though at same time I think anything else can't be possible.' Manjulika said.

'Same I also think.' Soma said.

'From childhood I thought how is world outside India and always had a dream to visit foreign countries.' Manjulika said.

'Not from childhood but from college life I developed a dream to visit at least one foreign country. Now dream is becoming true.' Soma said.

'Yes we will explore Europe.' Manjulika said in an excited, loud voice.

'Yes.' Madhulika and Soma said together in same excited and loud voice and after two seconds Manjulika heard ringtone of her mobile. Manjulika saw her neighbor friend Bristi was calling. Manjulika received the call, 'Hello Bristi!'

'Hello Manju! Where are you? In Delhi?'

'Yes, in Delhi.' Manjulika had shared her tour plan with Bristi.

'Have met with Sunil's family?'

'Yes today, has returned before some hours.'

'Okay so I have not wanted to call you now but has gotten an urgent problem. Can we talk for five minutes?'

'Sure, sure. I am free now. I am in hotel.'

'Okay it is about Shilpi.'

'Shilpi? What happened?' Shilpi was a girl who had worked as maid in Manjulika's house for two years before some years and she was working at Bristi's house that time, Manjulika knew that.

'Suddenly one thing has happened.'

'What?'

'You know Tarak Da came at our home for some works related to electricity.' Tarak was an electrician of Manjulika's neighbourhood.

'Okay.'

'I asked Shilpi to open the door and now Shilpi is telling after opening the door when Shlipi was bringing him to first floor he tried to hug Shilpi and now her boyfriend wants to bring police.'

'Did she say in front of Tarak Da.'

'No even same day, just after one week. I don't understand what is to do now.'

'After one week, why suddenly?'

'Taking salary.'

'Oh she was waiting for salary? And she did not shout at that time?'

'Yes I am also thinking it. We never heard anything bad about Tarak Da before. Don't know what is to do. So I want to know what kind of girl she is. Do you have any idea?'

'I saw her to talk with many boys. Whenever any young driver came from driver center at our home, she talked, she bought one second hand mobile from a driver giving half price.'

'Oh I also saw her to talk with drivers from driver center who came at our home.'

'Nothing wrong to talk but I find her way of talking seems like flirting and just think if a boy tries to hug any girl will she be able to control shouting, no I think. Instinctively she will shout, it will not be in her hand.'

'Yes, I also say that. But it is also a point why a girl says like this?'

'People say like this but there also can be many reasons. There is a chance she asked something or wanted to make relation but Tarak Da did not agree so she wants to take revenge.'

'Yes.'

'And how much I remember her boyfriend is not marrying her because she is divorcee and mother of one child so the mother of that boy does not want the marriage. There is a chance she said it to her boyfriend to tell how much problem she is getting to work at other's house now her boyfriend wants to come with police and now Shilpi can't tell truth.'

'Oh really? Her boyfriend does not marry her for this reason? Then there is a chance.'

'See this seems very logical why a girl says like this but boys are also not thinking when they get a chance to hug any girl.'

'Totally right. Anyway I shall talk with her.'

'If she brings police show those logics and if it will be needed call me.'

'Sure and anyway I have used your idea in my life.'

'Which idea?'

'One boys asked my number and I said, my number starts with eight and ends with zero, if you are smart find another numbers.'

Manjulika smiled and said, 'Nice and how did he react?'

'He sent smiley and now sometimes we talk on messenger.'

'Nice.'

'Okay will talk later. Have a nice and safe journey. Enjoy your tour.'

'Thanks.'

'Okay bye.'

'Bye.'

Manjulika cut the call and found Alberto's call, Manjulika went to balcony and received, 'Hello dear!'

'Hello darling, where are you?'

'Now in Delhi, have meet with Sunil's family today.'

'Oh nice, everything is fine?'

'Totally, just waiting for Europe tour.'

After a pause reply came, 'I am also very very excited to meet you. I can't believe I shall meet my love within some days.'

Manjulika smiled.

'Both of our parents have talked on phone and liked each-other, just hope everything will be fine and we will meet soon.' Alberto said.

'I also hope so dear.'

'Hope we will be able to marry soon.'

'Yes.' Manjulika said and smiled and said in mind, 'Then we will create our wonderland and will leave a dream life.'

'I love you dear.'

'I feel very happy hearing it.'

'Hope you will tell me I love you after we will meet.'

'I am just waiting to meet.' Manjulika smiled and said and found Soma to enter into balcony. Soma smiled little and said, 'Alberto?'

Manjulika smiled and nodded.

'Let me speak. Me and Madhulika also want to talk.' Soma said. Before that Madhulika and Soma talked with Alberto sometimes. 'Okay.' Manjulika smiled and said looking at Soma and said to Alberto on phone, 'Hello Alberto!'

'Yes dear.' Reply came from other side.

'My Didi and Soma Di want to talk with you.'

'Okay.'

'Okay I shall on the speaker.'

'Okay.' Alberto's reply came.

Manjulika looked at Soma and said, 'Let's go inside.' Soma smiled and said, 'Yes.' Manjulika and Soma went inside. Madhulika smiled looking at Manjulika. Manjulika sat on a chair and said looking at Madhulika, 'Okay I on the speaker, you both talk with him.'

'Okay.' Madhulika replied.

Soma sat on bed beside Madhulika. Manjulika on the speaker and informed Alberto. Madhulika started to talk with Alberto and Soma joined and Manjulika also joined. Soma took many tips for Europe about, transport, food, language and sightseeing and weather from Alberto then again Manjulika took the mobile and went to balcony and talked with Alberto some time more and cut the call after she remembered she had forgotten to take toothbrush. She informed Madhulika and Soma and got little scolding from Madhulika and they three went out for the nearest grocery store and bought toothbrush and three chocolates and returned to hotel.

12

Manjulika, Madhulika, their parents and Soma were standing inside the lift of the hotel in England where they had booked room to stay. 'Finally we have reached Europe.' Soma smiled and said. Manjulika, Madhulika, Rita and Animesh smiled. After lift was stopped in first floor they went near their rooms. Rita said, 'Anyone of you open our door. I am afraid to use key here.'

'Yes I am coming.' Madhulika said. Manjulika opened the door of one other room with Soma. After getting fresh Manjulika called Alberto and informed about reaching Europe. Then Manjulika went to do breakfast with her family. After finishing coffee taking the plate Manjulika went near the table of food items with Soma and said, 'Wow hash brown and baked beans. Sure I shall try it.'

'Me too.' Soma said from behind. Manjulika smiled and took two hash browns and some baked beans and some other items and went near her table and sat and tried hash brown at first. Soma joined her after some time. Madhulika finished her coffee and said, 'I am going to bring other items.'

'You can try hash brown, really nice.' Soma said.

'Yes really nice and you should try baked beans also. Nothing special but I think you should try.' Manjulika said.

'Okay.' Madhulika smiled little and said. Soma also smiled. Manjulika noticed her parents were going towards the table of food items. Manjulika said looking at Madhulika, 'Didi, Baba and Maa are going to bring foods please guide them.'

Madhulika smiled and said, 'Sure.' and left. Manjulika took one bite of hash brown, Soma also took one bite of hash brown and said, 'Really tasty yaar. I tried two times in our country but it was not that tasty.'

'Same experience, I also tried two times and it is far tastier.'

Soma took one more bite of hash brown and said, 'Once I wanted to try baked beans and saw in menu card of one restaurant but the price was too high and I felt baked beans does not worth it.'

Manjulika put little baked beans in mouth, took a pause and said, 'Actually I also found many items' price is too high in some restaurants and I think everywhere every restaurant should have option of half plates and quarter plates for every items so some people can try spending little price and rare anyone will waste anything.'

'Right.'

'Anyway coffee was also tasty.'

'Yes.' Soma replied and kept quiet few seconds and wiped tears. Manjulika noticed that and asked, 'Hey what happened?'

Soma kept quiet few seconds and wiped her tears once again and said, 'I remember my mother.'

Manjulika got puzzled for few seconds, did not understand what to say. Soma said, 'People say time is the greatest healer but my pain is increasing with time, day by day.' Manjulika looked at Soma with a sad face. Soma kept quiet few seconds and said, 'I wish I could bring my mother here.' Manjulika kept quiet few seconds then kept a hand on Soma's hand. Soma smiled little. Madhulika came near the table and sat on her chair then looked at the hand of Soma which Manjulika was keeping. Madhulika kept quiet few seconds and said, 'What happened?'

'Soma Didi is remembering her mother.' Manjulika said.

Madhulika looked at Soma with a sympathetic face. Manjulika left Soma's hand. Madhulika said, 'Kakima is always with you.'

Soma smiled little and said, 'I know and I contacted her once after that I feel it more but I wish I could bring her here.'

'May be she is here with us..., in this hotel. She can see us, just we can't see her.' Manjulika said again, 'Just you can't do photo season with her.'

'But I can't talk with her. Sometimes I really felt an urge to talk with her. After coming here I am feeling it more.' Soma said. Manjulika and Madhulika looked at each-other with sad faces.

'Be happy. If Kakima sees coming here you are not enjoying remembering her, she will feel bad.' Madhulika said.

Soma smiled little.

'So you just enjoy the tour.' Madhulika said. Manjulika took a bite of hash brown and continued eating. After break-fast Manjulika, Madhulika, their parents and Soma went for sightseeing and after visiting some places visited a branch of international eatery which was famous for burger. After that Manjulika, Madhulika and Soma bought three t-shirts, some pens and returned back to hotel. Being fresh lying on bed beside Manjulika, Soma said, 'I can't believe we have spent one day in London.'

'Same here.' Manjulika replied.

'I feel like dream came true.'

'Really.'

'I have enjoyed a lot.'

'Me too.'

Soma took a pause and said, 'But your real excitement is waiting for you.' Manjulika understood Soma was telling about Alberto. Manjulika gave a shy smile. After a pause Soma said, 'You know

now I think visiting foreign countries is also happened if it is written in your destiny.'

'Of-course.'

'Actually now I feel everything depends on our destiny.'

'Sure, not only every individual person's destiny, many things which are happening in this world are also pre-decided.'

'Right.'

'I was thinking before some days how world is changing that is also pre-decided.'

'Sure.'

'See day by day how dressing style is changing. Now any girl does not wear saree in college, boys left wearing dhuti-punjabi before [illegible]any years.'

[illegible]ht.'

[illegible]most everyone is changed. I heard before many years [illegible] was considered as bad thing as hard-drink in our country [illegible] almost all persons of our generation drink sometimes [illegible] houses parents and children taking hard-drinks

[illegible]es I think how people forget about past

[illegible]amilies you can find almost in every [illegible] name of till grandparents of past

[illegible] And some people have [illegible]rents and some have knowledge about grandparents' grandparents but I think any family can remember maximum twenty-five generations.'

'Right.'

'I think it happens because new generation will forget about old generations day by day it is also pre-decided.'

Soma smiled.

'Scientific invention is also pre-decided. We think scientists are inventing new new things but actually those things would be invented by them was pre-decided.' Manjulika said and smiled. Madhulika was playing game on mobile. She said, 'Please stop those philosophical discussion coming here.'

Manjulika and Soma smiled looking at each-other. After five seconds Soma said, 'Okay I am coming from washroom.'

'Okay.' Manjulika said.

Soma left the bed and went to washroom and came out after some time and just opening the door she said, 'Great…'

Manjulika and Madhulika looked at her with puzzled faces
Manjulika asked, 'What happened?'

'My period is started.' Soma replied.

'Oh no.' Manjulika said.

'Disgusting.' Soma replied. Madhulika kept looking at her
glum face. Manjulika asked, 'Your date was this time?'

Soma said, 'Yes but many times date does not match a
period even ten days later but this time just two d
Disgusting.'

Manjulika and Madhulika looked at each-other with gl

'My fate always betrays with me.' Soma said as
suitcase and took out packet of sanitary napkin Free
Manjulika said, 'Don't think always negative. Ma

like this. I think, if you think you can understand many positive things are also happened in your life.'

Soma smiled.

'Soma Di do you do shampoo after period?' Manjulika asked.

'No no not at all. I also don't do as Madhulika does not do.'

Madhulika smiled. Manjulika said, 'Yes we both don't do. I never did but I don't enter religious place or touch religious stuff.'

'Same here.' Soma said.

'I don't believe in fake chauvinism and feminism. I think any gender is not allowed to enter at religious places not taking bath.' Manjulika said.

'Yes right.' Soma said and went to washroom once again with a sanitary napkin in her hand and came out after some time. After some more talking Manjulika and Madhulika and Soma went to call Animesh and Rita for dinner. Animesh was wearing one formal pant and a t-shirt and Rita was wearing salwar-kamiz which they had been wearing in the time of sightseeing. Manjulika said, 'Baba and Maa I wanted to tell you something whole day.'

Rita and Animesh looked at her. 'You both are looking very nice. I have not seen you ever in this kind of dress.'Manjulika said.

'Yes really you both are looking nice, we saw Baba to wear formal pant with shirt but not with t-shirt and never Maa to wear salwar-kamiz.' Soma said.

'We will do photo season after dinner in balcony.' Manjulika said.

Animesh and Rita smiled looking at each-other. Manjulika, Madhulika, their parents and Soma went to do dinner in a restaurant of the hotel and tried buffet of dinner then returned in room and did photo session for almost half an hour before sleeping.

To be continued...